SORCERER'S WALTZ

SORCERER'S WALTZ

SCIONS OF MAGIC™ BOOK SIX

TR CAMERON   MICHAEL ANDERLE   MARTHA CARR

DISRUPTIVE IMAGINATION

Copyright © 2020 TR Cameron & Michael Anderle
Cover Art by Jake @ J Caleb Design
http://jcalebdesign.com / jcalebdesign@gmail.com
Cover copyright © LMBPN Publishing
A Michael Anderle Production

LMBPN Publishing
PMB 196, 2540 South Maryland Pkwy
Las Vegas, NV 89109

First US edition, March 2020
Version 1.01 May 2020
ebook ISBN: 978-1-64202-821-8
Print ISBN: 978-1-64202-822-5

THE SORCERER'S WALTZ TEAM

Thanks to the JIT Readers

Jeff Eaton
Nicole Emens
Larry Omans
Dorothy Lloyd
Deb Mader

If I've missed anyone, please let me know!

Editor
Skyhunter Editing Team

For those who seek wonder around every corner and in each turning page. And, as always, for Dylan and Laurel.

— *TR Cameron*

CHAPTER ONE

"What the hell did you say?" Caliste Leblanc, matriarch of House Leblanc—one of the nine noble families of New Atlantis—stared across the table that separated her from the man on the other side of the booth.

Wymarc Jehenel, patriarch of House Jehenel, laughed. His perfectly white teeth gleamed in contrast to his dark skin, the combination undeniably handsome. She'd been told he was considered the most handsome and most desirable bachelor in the city. While she could see the allure, her interest wasn't romantic.

At the moment, at least. But I could certainly choose worse.

His voice was low and sultry. "I said, rumor has it that Styrris Malniet is considering remarrying. Potentially the leader of another of the Nine."

She shook her head in disbelief. "Does that happen?"

He shrugged. "Not in my lifetime, certainly. You'd have to go back a fair way, probably." When he'd invited her out for a meal, she'd been more or less obligated to attend. She hadn't felt the need to dress up, but her great aunt Emalia had insisted. His button-down shirt shimmered in dark-purple, the only note of color in an otherwise black outfit. Cali had selected a deep scarlet dress with black accents over black leather leggings and her mother's boots, which she'd adored since the moment she'd first seen them. Her red curls were piled atop her head in something approximating fashion, again at her elder's urging. It was much more appropriate for a date than for a strategy session.

"So would they combine into a single house? Wouldn't that create a power vacuum?"

Wymarc chuckled but managed to avoid sounding condescending. *Good choice, buddy.* "I can't see old Styrris allowing that to happen. More likely, he's planning to absorb the other house."

Cali took a sip of her cider and returned the glass to the table. "So you're being clever by not revealing the name. You want me to guess, is that it?"

Her companion laughed and nodded. "Of course. Nothing comes for free in New Atlantis, you know that. Right now, the cost is merely a game."

She considered what she knew about the other houses. Most of them would be too entrenched and too proud to allow such a thing. She assumed Styrris would look for a matriarch, as his last spouse had been female. "It would have to be someone who doesn't support the Empress or is at least willing to turn. By your own words, that limits it to Surette, Devaux, or Cormier."

He took a sip of his ale and wiped his lips with the knuckle of a long finger. "That is logical. And Surette is led by a patriarch, so that one is less likely."

She nodded. "And Devaux is rather obvious since

they're publicly anti-Shenni. So, Cormier? But the Matriarch is only—what, twenty-eight? And Styrris is maybe ten decades older?"

For a moment, he looked thoughtful while he tapped a fingernail on the table. "About four—maybe four and a half. But yeah, it's a wide age gap. Quite a score for the old boy."

"Your chauvinism is showing." She gave him a withering look. "Try not to be a chucklehead."

Wymarc released the laugh he'd held. "You're so easy sometimes, Cali."

"That's only a rumor." The automatic response passed her lips without thought. She'd developed a wide repertoire of snarky comebacks while busking in Jackson Square, where the tourists seemed to enjoy trading barbs with the performers. It was a matter of busker pride to ensure the visitors always departed in defeat. "So, how likely is it? And what's the bigger strategy? Does he have allies ready to step in if Cormier is removed?"

"You'd have to assume so, right?" He shrugged. "It wouldn't be like him—or any of the Nine—to make such a move with the outcome left to chance."

Cali leaned back in the booth to allow the server to slide her dinner onto the table. She had ordered one of the local dishes, seafood pasta in a red sauce with spices she'd never had anywhere other than in the undersea city. Generally, she preferred what Wymarc derisively called "surface food," but this particular dish had grown on her. A grilled hunk of an unspecified animal or fish filled the plate that appeared in front of her dining companion. Her response was delayed by a sustained attack on her meal.

When she came up for air, she expelled a satisfied sigh. "So what's the reasoning behind it? Does he not have enough people to depend on in his house?"

The man across from her patted his lips with a black cloth napkin before he dropped it into his lap and picked his utensils up. He sectioned the remaining parts of his meal while he spoke.

"I doubt that's it. If I had to guess, he's found a way to turn your challenge into an opportunity to rally others against you and the Empress. And either the Cormier matriarch wasn't willing to join without a marriage or someone lower in that house has struck a deal and offered her as the prize."

She frowned. "So, despite the constant pretense of honor among the Nine, it's a facade."

He pointed his knife at her. "You have seen the light. Well done."

"Or, maybe, this is all an effort by you to win my support." She chuckled. "Wheels inside wheels."

Wymarc shook his head. "I prefer to be measured by my actions. I don't need anyone's help and if I did, I would be up-front about it."

Sure you would. When she'd first met the man, she would have attributed the comment to his true belief in his appeal. After spending time with him, she'd come to realize that while he wouldn't refrain from using his beauty as a tool, it wasn't all there was to him. At the same time, his commitment to working only at the surface level wasn't accurate either. "Of course you would." She deadpanned and waited for his response.

He stared at her and she kept her face blank. Finally, he grinned. "You're something, Caliste Leblanc."

Superficial conversation accompanied the rest of the meal and the dim surroundings of the restaurant afforded privacy they wouldn't have had closer to the city center. It had been his idea to come to the venue in the next-to-outermost section to evade the prying eyes that routinely watched the nightspots closer to the palace. She was definitely behind the times on information-gathering in New Atlantis, with only Emalia seeking knowledge on her behalf and not in any systematic manner.

Another thing I need to embrace unless I can find a way to bring this challenge to a premature end.

After dessert and coffee, she'd had enough of both her escort and being in public. If it wouldn't have been perceived as entirely rude, she would have portaled home and headed to bed. Instead, she stifled a yawn as they stepped out onto the road beyond the restaurant. New Atlantis' night had fallen while they dined and it was mostly dark, the only illumination a dim light that filtered from above and the occasional wrought iron lantern streetlight. Closer to the palace, the lamps were almost continuous. There, they were puddles of gray in a sea of shapes demarcated in shades of black.

The quiet click as the door closed was followed by a louder one that set her nerves afire—a deadbolt sliding home. She whispered, "Wymarc," and he nodded.

"I heard it too."

"Portal?"

He didn't have time to reply as a wave of bodies appeared at a run out of the darkness. She cursed and mentally commanded the scarlet and black bracelets she wore to transform into fighting sticks. They turned liquid and flowed over her hands to reform into the etched magical weapons Zeb had created for her.

She pointed at the figure in the lead but held her attack and yelled, "Hold or face the consequences."

Wymarc growled impatiently. "You can't reason with them. They're mercenaries. If they give up, they'll never be hired again." He threw a ball of fire at the center of the formation, and they parted to evade it but didn't lessen the speed of their approach one iota.

Thoughts flicked through her mind—*How does he know? Are they after me or him? How did they find us?*—but none of them mattered. She released the hold on her power and a force bolt traveled through her stick. The etched runes glowed for an instant before the magic exploded from the tip and pounded into the nearest enemy. The strength of the blast hurled him back into the darkness. She swung the stick toward the next but he had already begun his attack.

Lightning emerged from his fists as he raced toward her and the flares strobed the surrounding motion in her vision so it all seemed abstract and at a level removed from reality. She struck her sticks together in front of her to form an X, and her magic reached out to draw in the electrical assault and neutralize it against her weapons. When her attacker dropped the assault, she hurled the stick in her right hand at his face and skittered left to sidekick the foe who snuck in from that side.

Good try, chucklehead.

The force blast that struck her came as a total surprise and hurled her to bounce off the building and fall heavily.

Only her reflexive tuck protected her skull from smacking the restaurant wall.

Dammit. Nice trap. The first guy was the bait and I fell for it. She shook her head and pushed to her feet as Wymarc leveled two enemies with simultaneous blasts of shadow aimed at their heads. She ran to his side and discovered that while they'd dealt with the initial attackers, the others had arranged themselves into a semicircle with them in the center. At least a dozen still remained. If their foes were nonmagicals, those odds might be doable. This situation, however, was far more challenging.

She shouted, "Hey, hold up. Who's in charge here?" While she awaited their response, she sent a mental call across the city and received a wave of affirmation in reply. She smothered her smile at the eagerness that colored it.

One of the men stepped forward. He looked older with a black beard and mustache traced with gray hair. A small scar on his cheek gave him character. His features were hard and square, and his voice was equally solid. "That would be me."

Cali nodded. "And you know who I am?"

"Of course."

"Whatever you're being paid, I can pay more. I don't have as large a household to support as the…"

He responded with a thin smile but didn't end the sentence as she'd hoped. *Dammit.* Instead, he said, "What kind of people would we be if we gave our word and then abandoned our commitment for a better prize?"

With her eyebrow raised in challenge, she said, "Smart ones?"

Beside her, Wymarc sighed. "Now he'll say he couldn't

possibly, and you'll offer more, but he'll stand on his alleged honor, knowing there's no way he'd ever get a job again if he allowed a target to outbid his employer." He shook his head. "Let's cut to the chase. How about we do this two on two, Kreeson?"

The other man shrugged. "I can't do it, Wy. Promises were made."

She turned to her companion. "You know this guy?"

His chuckle was dark. "I know all kinds of people. He's a good drinking companion when he's not being paid to hurt me."

The mercenary leader coughed. "It's not you, Wy. It's her. You could take a walk."

Cali pointed a finger at him. "You, shut up and wait." She turned to Wymarc. "He's not wrong. I can probably beat them on my own. I'm not exactly helpless."

"There are three reasons I can't go. First, it would damage my reputation if word got out, and there's a whole restaurant full of cowards watching. Second, I invited you to this part of the city so technically, the situation is my fault."

He paused and it seemed like everyone waited in silence for his next words.

Finally, she asked, "And the third thing?"

He grinned. "This." He spun and launched two lines of shadow magic from his fists that met at the chest of the leader and blasted him out of sight.

CHAPTER TWO

The remaining mercenaries surged forward, several of those quicker on the uptake and a step ahead of their comrades. She felt the incoming surprise for them before she saw him and grinned as Fyre flashed through the pool of light to her left and sprayed a long line of frost across the front rank. The Draksa's magic coated them in ice and froze them in place like statues. Shouts and bolts of power sought him as he flew past but managed only to illuminate his gorgeous metallic scales, now fully a blend of the Leblanc house colors—turquoise and red with occasional lines of deep black.

She spoke into his mind, "Great job, buddy," and amusement flowed to her in reply. Wymarc had clearly been surprised by the dragon lizard's appearance, as he was a full two steps behind when she crossed in front of him to attack the enemies on the right-hand side of the formation. They spun bolts of power at her and she slapped them away with her sticks and channeled a touch of magic to attract and absorb the enemy attacks.

When Nylotte had taught her the skill, the Drow had scoffed at the fact that she didn't know it already and had promised that in future sessions, she'd teach her to use her enemy's magic as fuel for her own. When she'd told Emalia about it, her great aunt had only shrugged and said there were as many approaches to magic as there were people, and she'd do well to learn from everyone she could.

Reflection time ended when she reached hand-to-hand combat range. She channeled her motion into a front kick with her right leg and drove her reinforced heel into her opponent's sternum. His padded jacket prevented him from going down but the look on his face showed he'd lost at least some of his breath. As soon as her foot landed, she lifted it again, spun back, and whipped her sticks at head height. The man on her left managed to raise an arm to block but the velocity of the weapons snapped his forearm with a loud crack. He fell, cradling it as he moaned in pain.

Fyre screeched when he darted in again and locked another of the mercenaries in a sheath of ice. Wymarc tumbled into a pool of light as he dodged a fireball and straightened quickly with daggers made of shadow magic in his hands. He became a blur of motion as he alternately kicked and slashed with the blades of power. His opponent fell and blood welled from a jagged line that stretched from his cheek to his temple. He looked at his fighting partner in triumph before he catapulted to slam into the wall of the restaurant and slumped dazedly on the street.

Fyre screamed and dove at the duo that now approached her, but they turned together and fired magic at him—a cone of shadow from the first and a net made out of electricity from the other.

Dammit. Why did it have to be lightning? Cali instructed the Draksa to withdraw with a telepathic message and centered herself physically and mentally. One of the two was Kreeson, who had recovered from Wymarc's attack. The other was a woman of about the same age, her long hair also streaked with gray and her features hard and unyielding. Her voice, though, contained all the melody her leader's lacked. "Well, Caliste of House Leblanc, the tales we were told of your prowess were certainly true."

"Word travels fast." She gestured at the fallen and ice-encased mercenaries around them. "Are we done here? Because, frankly, if I'd known this would be a double date, I probably would have declined."

The other woman laughed. "No, I'm afraid our instructions were clear."

"And those were?"

Her opponent grinned and Kreeson matched the expression. He said, "Ask again when it's done—if you still can—and maybe I'll tell you."

They separated and put a little distance between them so she couldn't catch them both with a single attack, and she let the fireball she'd been building fizzle.

I can't use my light charm. There would be too much collateral damage in the restaurant and I have no way to warn Wymarc. It's time for an old-fashioned ass-kicking, then.

She launched herself into a run at the woman and pumped magic into her muscles to increase her speed. As always, the rush of power that surged through her body made her wish it would never leave, exactly as Emalia had warned it would. She had no mental bandwidth to worry about that, though, as her foe created a rope of lightning

11

with a ball of the same energy on the end. With almost nonchalant skill, she whipped it around her head and released it.

The orb traveled far faster than physical muscles could have driven it, and Cali narrowly avoided it with a deep backbend and slide. She'd anticipated the move accurately, but her enemy vaulted up and over her an instant before she could sweep her legs out from under her. With a muttered curse, she forced herself up, dropped her left stick, and spun in time to create a force buckler over her left hand. She interposed it in the path of the lightning ball when it was a foot away from her face and managed not to smack herself in the head from the impact, but only barely.

Thankfully, both her opponent's hands were occupied with her weapon, which left her nothing to defend herself with when Cali stretched her stick out and delivered a blast of force from it. At the last instant, she lowered her aim from the woman's face to her abdomen. The blow knocked the wind out of her and her out of the fight.

The distraction allowed Kreeson to find an angle, though, and she growled through the pain when a bolt of shadow struck her. Her dress offered zero protective capabilities, and the impact was sufficient to lance misery through all the ribs on that side. She gasped in shock, forced herself to move, and flung her body forward to avoid the second attack but lost her remaining stick in the process. She sectioned off the part of her mind that felt the agony and used the rest to summon a force shield that was taller and wider than she was and slid it between herself and her foe. He battered it with magical attacks as he approached, but she was equal to them.

His grin grew as he closed. "You were all that they said you'd be. The company's reputation will grow as a result of this battle, our prices will increase, and my life will be better. I guess I owe you thanks."

Cali shook her head. "I'm not sure if you have them down here, but up on the surface, we have these things called chickens. They come from eggs."

He looked at her in confusion. "What?"

She shrugged. "It's an old phrase. Don't count your chickens before they're hatched." She directed power into her muscles again and sprinted toward him with the shield extended before her. He was still confused when the slab of force thumped into him and he reeled. She dropped the magic and spread her open hands. A moment later, both her sticks slapped into her palms. She used him as a targeting dummy and struck along each attack vector in sequence, her magically enhanced speed a little too rapid for his attempts at defense.

By the time she stopped, he staggered on his feet, his arms hanging at his sides. She drove a spinning back kick into his chest and he fell. "Lock 'em down, buddy," she called, and Fyre swooped in and coated all the fallen mercenaries with magical frost.

After a hasty scrutiny of the area to confirm that the danger was over, she strode to Wymarc, who was seated against the wall and laughed softly. He winced with every chuckle that escaped him. "Chickens," he choked. "Really?"

With a grin, she retrieved the flat plastic tube that lay under the strap that rested around her hips beneath her dress. Her thumb popped the top, and she placed it to his lips. "Shut up and drink."

He obeyed, and his features eased as the healing potion worked its magic. She gave herself a pat on the back for the foresight to realize she'd need alternate methods to carry her magical tools when circumstances forced her out of her everyday wardrobe or fighting clothes. Satisfied that he was on the mend, she pulled him to his feet and he surveyed the mercenaries with a shake of his head.

"How long until the ice wears off?"

Fyre landed gracefully beside her with a flutter of wings and looked pleased with himself.

"About thirty minutes or so," she answered, "based on past experience. Less if any managed to get their magic working before they were hit. Power tends to loosen its hold."

Wymarc nodded. "Will they be okay?"

Cali shrugged. "There won't be damage from the ice if that's what you mean. At least a few of them had broken bones, I think, but none are in imminent danger as far as I noticed."

"Same here. Kreeson isn't all that bad, compared to other mercenaries. The Nine wouldn't lower themselves to hire the worst ones, of course, unless an open war broke out. But still, we'd better keep our eyes open. If they were willing to hire one company, they'll be willing to hire another."

"I guess we should take advantage of the opportunity to acquire intelligence, then." She walked to where the mercenary leader lay frozen on the ground and knelt beside him. Carefully, she channeled fire into her hand to warm it but didn't release the power. She placed her palm on his cheek to melt the ice there and continued the process until his face was free. He snarled and struggled to no avail, and she flicked his nose with her middle finger.

"Hey, stupid, knock it off. Answer a couple of questions and you and your people will live. Otherwise, I'll open a portal to the World in Between and throw you through." It was an empty threat as she had no idea how to do that and had only heard of the place while doing research in the Magical Library in New Orleans.

But he doesn't know that. She made sure her face reflected none of her ignorance or hesitation.

His eyes widened at the threat, which suggested that he too knew of the World in Between. He tried and failed to nod because of the ice and choked out a harsh, "Ask."

"Were your orders to kill me?"

"No. Only to hurt you. A lot." If she'd hoped for regret, he apparently had none to offer.

"Okay. That gets you a little credit with me, anyway. Now, the important question. Who hired you?"

Kreeson's eyes flicked over her shoulder as Wymarc stepped beside her. Her partner said, "Tell the truth, old friend. I'll make it easier for you. It was Cormier, wasn't it?"

The mercenary closed his eyes and muttered, "Yes. Cormier."

Cali patted his icy chest. "Good boy. Well done." She stood, considered the option of having Fyre freeze him again, but decided against it. Instead, she turned to her companion with a goofy grin. "You sure do know how to show a girl a fun time."

He looked stunned for a moment before he broke into a smile. "I guess I do at that. Who knew that House Cormier would provide such an interesting and interactive adventure for us? I must be sure to write them a note of thanks."

"More like burn their house down around them," she muttered, too low for anyone else to hear. Then, she answered, "It would probably be best if we both did to make sure they know they've annoyed two houses rather than only one."

He turned and offered her his arm, which was silly, but she took it with a shake of her head. "So, do you fancy an evening stroll through the worst parts of town?" he quipped. "After this, I can't imagine we'll find anything truly dangerous awaiting us. The mercenary companies tend to keep the field clear when they're working. It's kind of a common respect thing."

"Until they wind up on opposite sides and have to try to kill one another, is that it?"

Her companion shrugged. "Such is the life of the soldier for hire."

Cali sighed. "I would have said there was no place on Earth stranger than New Orleans. But once again, New Atlantis proves me wrong." She pointed toward the palace. "Home, Wymarc. Fyre, get up high and watch for trouble."

He ran, launched himself into the air, and soared gracefully upward. She would have preferred to portal but appearances had to be maintained, and a casual saunter to House Leblanc would show exactly how unaffected she was by the assault.

And, if my enemies misinterpret that action as proof that the incident has been forgiven or forgotten, so much the better.

CHAPTER THREE

U sha tapped her foot in time to the fast Jazz music coming from the stage. The crowd at the Shark Nightclub was decent for a Tuesday night, and the band was a local group that had begun to attract a following. Even though the club had always been the headquarters for the Atlantean gang in New Orleans, she had worked hard to turn it into a real and profitable venue during her years at the helm.

Its popularity was assured by the fact that her bartenders made killer rum drinks, and she was on her third Pina Colada of the evening. The alcohol took the edge off everything around her and made the colors wash together and the sounds of the audience blur into that of the instruments. But even all that weight on the positive side of the scale was unable to completely banish the concerns that pressed on the opposite end of the pivot. And, like her moods, the scale swung wildly in judgment of her plans, each one good for a moment and bad in the next.

She was aware she was being maudlin and sighed.

Sensing its approach, she'd done all she could to avoid the mood—put her brightest dress on, spent time on her hair, and surrounded herself with the things she usually liked. But the pressure was unremitting and her attempts to evade it were doomed to failure over a long enough timeline.

The good feelings might have lasted a little longer, though. That would have been nice, Universe.

The Atlantean gang leader drained the last of her drink and gestured at the bartender. The woman approached immediately and looked fantastic in her deeply plunging scarlet blouse and black leather pants. The watchword for all the workers at the Shark was, "If you have it, flaunt it," and it applied equally to all genders and positions. She wanted her customers to bask in the sensations around them and forget their troubles for a time. Now and then, she thought she might truly enjoy owning a bar as her sole vocation, but those moments were fleeting. She craved more than such a solitary pursuit offered. The server's voice was low and sultry as she indicated the empty cup. "Another?"

Usha shook her head. "Coke, ice, and the biggest glass you have." It was time to get her mind back in the game. Applause rang out as the band finished the song, and she took a moment to survey the room and enjoy the smiles on so many faces. She took them as a testimony of the atmosphere she'd created for her guests. The drink arrived, and she drained half while she held her hand up to keep the woman from leaving.

"Refill." The bartender laughed and moved to comply

with the request. Usha stood, accepted the full glass, and headed to her office in the rear of the club.

———

She'd worked at her desk for an hour and a quarter when Danna finally appeared. They didn't have a set meeting time, merely an agreement that they would end their workday together in the Shark. Occasionally, other pursuits would take precedence and they'd miss one but most often, they met as planned. Her second in command wore a dark scarlet suit, the color surprising enough that it required a moment to take it in. She wore black against it —shirt, tie, and shoes—and her shortish hair was spiked upward tonight. Usha grinned. "Clubbing?"

The woman groaned and moved toward the couches, and she rose to join her. Soon, they had settled in their usual positions, seated diagonally across from one another on the comfortable furniture. Her subordinate sighed and leaned her head back to stare at the ceiling.

"The problem isn't the personal delivery to our best clients." She was referring to the distribution of Zarcanum, their drug tailored to magicals. The demand often exceeded the supply, and the need to be very careful with the product lest it be stolen and copied required her second's direct involvement. *It won't last, but we'll stretch it out for as long as we can.* "It's the fact that they want to talk. And talk. And talk."

Usha laughed. "They take pleasure in your company, Danna, as do I."

The other woman shook her head and closed her eyes.

"It's about being seen, for them. The longer they're in the presence of our people, the more social lift they get among their friends."

"That is mostly true, although it's not about being in a random person's presence but being in yours. I've heard the words—both shouts and whispers—praising you. I'm sure the suit increased your visibility tonight as well, which means you're playing the game perfectly."

She snorted. "I wore it because Winston likes his women in red. He didn't squeal when I told him the cost had gone up. It was a small price to pay."

The leader nodded. "Good thinking. Sadly, that won't work with everyone. But there's nothing to be done. Demand outstrips supply. It's the free market, baby."

Danna laughed. "Indeed. The rest of the deliveries were equally predictable. Kisses, hugs, and handshakes—again, a small price to pay for the money they hand over oh so willingly."

"Do you need a drink?" She gestured to the bar cart in the corner.

"Sweet heaven, no." They laughed together. "Every delivery requires a drink, of course. If not for a little boost of magic here and there, they would have had to drag me into the building to talk to you."

"Been there. It's better than digging ditches, though."

"Definitely." The woman lowered her gaze to meet her superior's. "So, what's up? You're not quite yourself."

"You know me that well, do you?" The peevish comment escaped unintentionally and she waved a hand to dismiss it. "Yeah, I know you do, so ignore that. It's been a difficult evening. I had too much time in my own head."

"Well, if you want to get out and join us on the deliveries again, you're always welcome."

Usha was sure she hadn't imagined the hint of advice-giving in her tone. It was true, though. She had been cooped up inside the club more or less constantly, except for occasional trips to visit the Empress. *Which are far fewer and more between than I'd like.* She shook her head. "I'm needed here. Plotting and planning, the spider monitoring her web."

"It's your curse to be so brainy." The sarcasm was delivered perfectly, and they both broke into laughter.

"You're such a wench. You're lucky you dress so well or you'd be out on your behind."

"I'm sure I could find someone to take my behind—and the rest of me—in."

She shook her head. "I surrender. I'm entirely too tired to be a worthy opponent." She took a deep breath to steady herself. "It's time to shift into the endgame."

Danna had entered her apartment building under the watchful eye of one of the Atlantean gang members. She could have portaled but Usha believed in maintaining an image, and that included expensive cars with drivers. She claimed it was good for the new recruits, too, to spend time in the presence of the leaders. Especially the men, who sometimes took longer than expected to fully come around to the idea that the top two positions had been earned by women because of their abilities and nothing more.

She climbed the stairs as quickly as her fancy black heels would allow. As soon as she had closed and locked the doors, she pressed the switch to trigger the lights to perform their nighttime routine. Ozahl had put the system together for her. A small computer attached to wireless sockets would play one of six sequences to make it look like she was still present. Before the lamp that suggested she was walking to the bedroom activated a minute later, the space was empty.

Less than a second later, she materialized in the single place in Ozahl's apartment where the wards would recognize her and permit her access, a walk-in closet. The motion-sensing light slowly illuminated, and she chuckled again at the fact that her partner had literally hidden her in a closet. She shook her head, pulled the door open, and stepped out into the bedroom.

Once she'd changed into comfortable clothes, she fell onto the king-sized mattress and sighed with pleasure to finally be off her feet. A light doze crept up on her and sucked her in. When she awoke, it was to her lover's lips on hers. They spent time wrapped in each other's arms and reveled in the closeness. Eventually, he shifted to lay on his back and she put her head on his chest.

Her voice was soft when she spoke as the atmosphere seemed to require it of her. "The gang is ready to make its move."

His breath hitched for a moment before he blew it out with a satisfied sound. "It's about time."

Danna gave a small but heartfelt laugh. "Right? I thought I would lose my mind."

"What's the plan?"

"It's a good one. It would be, coming from Usha. First, we'll begin to pull back the drug supplies, both the one for magicals and the one for humans. Word on the street will blame the Zatoras in general and Rion Grisham in particular."

She felt him nod. "That's a smart ploy, playing to public opinion. It's a shame we can't tell her what we're up to and use that clever mind. We'll make it up to her after, though."

Danna was silent for almost a minute. If she hated anything about the plans she'd made with Ozahl, it was the knowledge that her boss and best friend would inevitably be hurt by them, potentially grievously. She'd accepted the necessity of it long before but it nonetheless still wounded her anew each time she realized what their ambitions might cost Usha.

But after, when we have our own noble house, she will see what we did was for the greater good. And we can take care of her for the rest of her life.

Her partner interrupted her train of thought. "So, what then?"

"The main objective is to remove one of Grisham's lieutenants. It's our guess he'll feel the need for a funeral, something big and noticeable, if that were to occur. Does that agree with what you know about him?"

"Yeah." He sounded thoughtful. "Especially if someone further down the chain dropped the suggestion in his ear. I can make that happen. How will you do it?"

She chuckled. "Well, that's where you come in."

Laughter accompanied his reply. "Oh, is it? Okay, I think I can come up with an idea or three. What's Plan B?"

"Ugly. Plan B is ugly for everyone. Let's not talk about that right now."

His frown could be clearly felt in the way his body tensed under her. "Fine. Keep your secrets. But give me this, at least. Are you safe?"

Danna sighed. "Only time will tell, my love. Only time will tell."

CHAPTER FOUR

R ion Grisham wasn't at his best in the afternoon. Truly, he hit his stride at the start of the evening and held it into the early morning. But some things had to be done outside normal hours for the sake of secrecy. And today's conversation had to remain entirely secret lest his complicated plan go awry.

He strode into the back room of a restaurant they'd never used before, where his three lieutenants awaited him. They all nodded a greeting, which he returned briskly. Colin Todd, the besuited man who most resembled a handsome accountant, was as immaculate as always. Ozahl, his pet mage, was even more sloppily dressed than usual in loose black jeans and an oversized blue denim work shirt. Despite the man's appearance, he had complete confidence that the magical had searched for and eliminated any arcane surveillance, exactly as Todd would have done with the physical kind. His third underling wore an ill-fitting dark suit that his muscles distorted at the biceps and thighs.

The Zatora leader took his seat at the top of the table, with the humans on his left and the mage on his right. He noticed that the latter had a mole growing on his cheek and shook his head. *He can look any way he likes, and this is what he chooses.* Ozahl's ability with illusion was unmatched in Grisham's experience, not that he was an expert. He took what he could get, and the list of magicals willing to betray their own kind on behalf of a human criminal organization was as small as one would expect. He counted himself lucky to have the magical under his command.

It didn't alter the fact that he disliked the man or that he had put feelers out for a possible replacement. While Ozahl met and sometimes exceeded expectations, there was something about him that made it difficult to trust him fully. His boss had long since developed a nagging instinct that the man would somehow betray him but until he'd found a way to resolve the situation, he intended to make full use of what the magical had to offer. And, of course, to watch him closely while he did so.

He paused when the food arrived. His underlings always handled the orders and knew his preferences. The lamb chop that appeared in front of him looked amazing, and he took the first mouthfuls with relish and enjoyed the simple pleasure of eating. He tried to take his time with at least one meal a day and to keep his obsessive mind from grinding over the same thoughts again and again. Today, though, it didn't seem to work. It was far too big a day to permit distractions. He sampled the side dish of pasta, which was utterly average, and swallowed a few large sips of the red wine at his right hand. Finally, he put his utensils down and gazed at his people.

"So. The time has come. We will not wait any longer. The damn Atlanteans are squeezing us out of our own territory, and the doubly damned magical council has involved themselves more and more. We knew they were protecting the girl, but it appears they're doing more than that. We have it on good authority that they intend to attack us."

His people looked confused, and rightfully so. He'd made up the story to justify his desire to punch the magical community squarely in the teeth. *But they don't need to know that.*

Ozahl asked, "What authority is that?" His tone was mild but Grisham still heard the challenge in it.

He replied with a grin. "You're not the only one with sources, my friend. The little birds, they speak to me." He gestured around him and the men on his left laughed. "In any case, I am convinced we need to deal with both of them—now and decisively."

Jack Strang flexed his muscles, and his boss was certain the suit would surrender to the pressure. His voice was appropriately deep. "Hell yeah, boss. It's about time."

Todd nodded. "Past time, if you ask me." Both of their heads swiveled to regard the mage, who replied with a sigh.

"Cool. If it's time, it's time. What's the plan?"

The Zatora leader showed his teeth in a grin. "First, we gather intel. I want to know everything about the witch who leads the Atlanteans. Where she eats, where she sleeps, and if she has friends or family. The same applies to the one who's not sure if she's a boy or a girl." The humans laughed at the reference, but the mage merely maintained the same expression, locked somewhere between doubt and acceptance. "Todd, Strang, that's your task. Ozahl, you find out who our easiest target on the council is—the higher the better. Obviously, you'll lead that part of it."

The magical sat straighter and took a sip from the wine in front of him, then deliberately cut and ate a piece of his steak before he replied. "Obviously, but it's probably best if I'm there for both, don't you think? It would be a huge mistake to underestimate the Atlanteans because they're women."

Grisham stared at him. "I don't underestimate anyone, Ozahl. But thanks for the advice." The rebuke had no effect and simply slid off the man like everything else seemed to. But the others would receive a lesson, both about their boss's unwillingness to accept backtalk and about their fellow's weak efforts to confront him. "Now, let's finish our meal, have dessert, and talk about how we'll destroy these bastards for good."

Ozahl was in an uncharacteristic rage, although he hid it behind an illusion of normality, this one physical discipline rather than magical talent. In his head, he screamed at the memory of Grisham before he launched a wall of blades at the man.

Too bad it's only a dream. For the moment.

He'd said his farewells to the others outside the restaurant doors and found a nearby vacant alley. A portal took him to another part of the city, where he emerged from the shadows across from one of the nightclubs his most trusted helpers frequented.

His text had brought no response, which was usually the case when they were at the Rexy. It was arguably a dance club, with the requisite go-go girls dancing in cages mounted on pedestals above the dangerously packed dance floor. The large bar that filled the entry area was seven-deep, and the music throbbed and the hip-hop drums made his teeth ache.

After a moment, he decided his quarry would be on the upper level, and he threaded his way through the dancers to reach the stairs. They were guarded by two men in tight t-shirts and jeans. Their heavy boots looked like they had seen action already that night, to judge by the drops of red that glistened on them. He inclined his head toward the second floor, and the nearest guard stared at him. With a sigh, the mage slid a hand into his back pocket and pulled out a twenty-dollar bill. He trickled power into the man that made him see it as a hundred and suddenly, the path was open before him.

As he climbed the staircase slowly, he let his senses stretch ahead to seek any anomalies or dangers that might await him. Nothing returned to him and he mounted the top step with a sense of satisfaction. The music was muted there, reflected away by suspended panels that bounced the sound waves in different directions. To the left and the right were service bars, and private booths lined the walls that led toward the front of the room. Red leather and black wood, they were filled with the club's more affluent patrons who were served by go-go dancers awaiting their shift in the cages.

None of that mattered to him. A search in both directions revealed his quarry at the far end of the right side. Ozahl strode to their table, which they shared with four others. An open bottle of Gray Goose and numerous shot glasses littered the surface before them. He waved as he arrived and the duo sent their guests away.

Once they were gone, he slid into the booth beside the man. He was in his usual business casual look, with straight hair swept carefully to the side, an expensive watch, khakis, and a button-down. As long as you didn't look into his eyes, you might even buy it. The blonde woman stared at him with the look she sometimes got as if she considered making a move on him but realized it was a bad idea. He had no interest in anyone other than Danna at the moment and couldn't be bothered to pretend, even though Lila's flawless good looks drew attention to one degree or another

"So, any success?" he asked.

She shrugged. "We broke up a couple of Atlantean drug deals but they faded rather than fought."

The man nodded. "It's become boring. They're all about the long game, apparently."

"Yeah, well, it turns out Grisham isn't. We need to work on some stuff."

Both gazes swiveled to stare at him. Dalton said, "We'll finally attack the Atlanteans,?"

The mage nodded. "But not only them. Our friend Rion has decided it's time to take on everyone, all at once."

The woman turned her laugh into a cough. "That's...unsound."

"Yeah, but it's what the boss wants."

She shook her head. "What do you need us to do?"

"Two things, both more important than anything you have going. When this is over, I'll cover any losses you incur and add extra." While the Zatora crime syndicate paid its soldiers, these two were in it for the bigger scores, usually whatever was removed from a beaten or killed target. They nodded in agreement. "The first thing is that one of you needs to keep an eye on the enemy leader whenever she's awake. Her name is Usha. Do whatever you can to make sure you track her movements. We need to put together a picture of her life."

"So we plan to hit her?" Dalton asked,

Ozahl sighed. "That's Grisham's plan. I'm not sure it's a great idea, even if aiming for the head holds some appeal. Eliminating her support and negotiating with her might be the better play. We'll see how it develops. For now, though, for sixteen hours a day or so, you stick with her. Once we have a sense of her routine, we can bring in lower-level people to take over."

The woman laughed. "And in the wide swath of free time you've left us?"

He gave her a thin grin. "Investigate the magical council. I'll do the same and I'll share whatever I find with you. We're looking for the weak link, either the person whose removal will cause the most chaos or the one who's easiest to get alone. Hell, both, actually. The more we can discover, the better."

Lila stared at him for a long minute. "You're on board with this, are you?"

The mage chuckled. "You know me too well. I'll be honest, I'm not sure yet. There are pluses and minuses. My concerns are the same as they've always been—how we can get the most reward for the least risk. A big strike has the potential for the right ratio but only if we totally control the scenario. That's why I need you both on the job."

With another faint smile, he stood. "Tomorrow's soon enough, though. Enjoy your evening." He passed the other four people as they returned laughing to the table and shook his head. The two were skilled, dependable, and entirely hedonistic in their downtime. They were as far as could be from the discipline and control he and Danna displayed.

For the moment. Eventually, our time will come, and our new lives will make everyone around us envious.

As he stepped onto the street, Ozahl sighed and muttered under his breath. "Now all I need to do is decide which of the boss's helpers needs to die and how best to do it. Easy-peasy." He strode into the darkness, deep in thought.

CHAPTER FIVE

A giant yawn escaped Cali as she stepped off the final stair that separated her second-floor bedroom from the level that held the all-important coffee maker. She padded down the hall with her arms stretched high overhead and winced at the snap from her back. "Ow."

A voice from the kitchen asked, "Ow, what?" and she entered with a smile for her great aunt. Emalia was seated at the rectangular table with a teapot and mug nearby. In front of her was the coded book her parents had left in their bunker. The sight of it sparked hope but she pushed it down and headed to the cupboard.

A minute later, she sank into the chair across from the older woman and sipped from the delightfully bitter brew in her cup. With a frown, her companion suggested, "You should really drink tea. It replenishes your power."

She laughed. "It already feels like it might burst out of me at any moment. I don't think I can handle any more right now."

"We'll add that to the list of things to work on during

our training session," Emalia replied. "But first, we need to talk about information I've uncovered."

"Will I be happy?"

"A little yes, a little no. Such is life, Caliste."

The sudden formality suggested it would likely be more no than yes. Her great aunt tended to rely on distance when forced to deliver bad news. She, on the other hand, was a rip-off-the-Band-Aid-fast kind of person.

Fyre padded into the room and looked at them both before he chose a place under the table without speaking. He bumped her legs repeatedly, and she pictured him turning like a cat to find the right place to lay down in as if one section of the floor was somehow different from the other. The image dispatched her worry.

As long as I have amazing friends like Emalia, Fyre, Zeb, and Tanyith in my life, everything will be fine. Her internal voice prodded her as to why Wymarc wasn't on that list. *Shut up, you. Me. Whatever.*

"So, spill it, woman." Her grin rendered the comment playful instead of demanding.

Emalia nodded. "The good news first. I've discovered the location of another shard and have a line on yet one more."

Instantly, her smile widened and her words tumbled out in a rush. "That's fantastic! Where is it? How did you find it? Where's the other piece?"

Her great aunt chuckled. "Settle down, Caliste. The first is on Earth, in a museum."

Cali slapped her palms on the table. "All right. Road trip, Fyre." The Draksa snorted from below but an enthusiasm that matched hers flowed across the connection between them.

The older woman shook her head. "Where you're going, you can't use roads. Well, not all the way. It's in France but I'm not positive where yet. That will require research I'm not able to do here."

Cali nodded. The Internet had not reached New Atlantis. Sometimes, technologies would work inside the city—like the coffee maker or the lanterns outside—but she generally assumed they were magicked somehow. Privately, she found the overlaps of magic and technology entirely disconcerting, probably because she didn't fully understand either side of the equation. "I'll ask Scoppic for an assist. I'm sure he can help me find the right location."

"Yes. That is a good plan. Okay...now, the bad news. The book has comments about each of the other houses in here. Certainly, there might be more that I haven't yet decoded, but long story short, you shouldn't trust any of them. Your parents sought alliances when their troubles began and discovered that none of the Nine could be relied upon. They had a little more confidence in some rather than others but overall, the sense is that each is solely out for themselves. A house at risk of defeat and dissolution is more likely to bring them as attackers than defenders."

A chill swept through her, and she forced out the words she really didn't want to say. "Even House Jehenel?"

Emalia offered her a sympathetic smile. "Even House Jehenel. For what it's worth, they were not identified as enemies, only as non-allies. And there's every possibility that things could have changed since then."

"But no guarantee. I get it. Not a problem. What else?"

Her great aunt winced slightly. "The Empress also cannot be trusted."

Cali laughed. "That one's easy. I already don't trust her."

"It's more than that. You should consider her your enemy until she proves not to be, according to your parents' notes."

She took a large sip of her cooling coffee and sighed. "So, basically, assume everyone in New Atlantis wants to destroy me." The woman nodded. "Got it." Her good mood had evaporated, so the next words from her companion's mouth were both a positive and a negative.

"Okay. That's done. Let's go train."

The outbuilding had been recently cleaned. The room they were in had doubtless been the main chamber—probably a living room, although it was empty of furniture. It sparkled with the wood polished and any dust eliminated, and even the air held a fresh scent.

"Did you do this?" Cali asked.

Emalia shook her head. "I hired workers. While the people in the dome seem mostly allergic to hard work, the same is not true of those in the surrounding parts of the city. They came highly recommended."

"Jenkins?"

She nodded. "Jenkins. He's been an incredible help in numerous areas. I still can't imagine what kind of personality would want to continue in that particular role beyond their contracted term, but we're lucky to have him."

"Family," she told the woman. "He did it for his family back then but now, we're his family."

"I'm sure that's it."

"If you can find any way to reward him or his descendants, please do. You know, in your spare time."

The older woman laughed. "Right. So, speaking of time, we should quit wasting it. Let's work first on your control of the power inside you and see if there's a way to stretch the bubble that holds it in."

The half-hour that followed was mostly meditative as Cali tried to accomplish that goal while the soft voice of her great aunt guided her along each step. More than once, it occurred to her that Emalia's dedication to family was as substantial as Jenkins'. By the end of it, she'd managed to decrease the pressure a little to the approval of her teacher.

"Good work. Between now and our next lesson, you should try to summon more power from within. The tea will help."

She nodded and stood with a groan when her muscles protested. The day after the fight had been the most painful but lingering soreness remained that remaining seated for thirty minutes had exacerbated. She bent forward and put her hands on the floor to release another series of cracks from her back. "Ow."

Her companion laughed. "So, do you still want to work on lightning?"

"Yep. Ever since I fought those lightning lines, I've wanted some of my own. Plus, blasting a number of people at once with electricity holds appeal. That would have been good the other night."

"Well, then, let's get to it. You'll recall that it will require a great deal of mental discipline, right?"

Cali stuck her tongue out at the grinning older woman. "Yes, and I also recall telling you I could handle it. So, how about you teach, teach?"

Emalia pointed to the wardrobe that had been selected as a sacrificial target for their practice session. She closed her eyes for a moment and when she opened them, a thin line of power extended from her finger to strike the wood and immediately scored it. Rotation drew a full circle about a foot in diameter.

When she released the magic without any visible effort, Cali sighed. "Lightning?"

Her mentor nodded. "Yep. Very finely controlled. You shouldn't expect to reach this level of precision for some time, though."

She released another sigh. "Okay, way to destroy all the enthusiasm I had for this. Has anyone ever complimented your teaching? No? I wonder why."

The jibe drew a laugh. "When your mouth works, your brain doesn't. So perhaps you should stop talking and think. Imagine the lightning as a chaotic power that you have to force into submission and confine into the narrowest channel you are able to create. It will increase the impact of the magic as well as keep you from hitting anyone you don't intend to."

"Okay. I can do that." She nodded, closed her eyes, and sought inside for the path that would let her power emerge as lightning rather than force, fire, or muscle magic. When she found it, she released it in a thin stream and imagined it stretching to the wardrobe. She opened her eyes and grimaced at the sparkles that wreathed her hand but didn't go anywhere else.

"You made a good start," Emalia encouraged. "Now push. You're throttling it too much."

Cali obeyed and forced the lightning out of her fist. It burst free in an unexpected surge and she corralled it frantically into something roughly cone-shaped. It struck the target, the rest of the wardrobe, and the wall above and to either side. She dispelled it in a panic when she felt even her minimal control slipping.

Frustration swamped her and she turned her face to the ceiling and shouted, "Damn it to hell."

Her great aunt put a hand on her shoulder and she flinched. "It's okay, Caliste," the woman said soothingly. "You're improving. I told you it would take longer than you wanted it to. This is a very challenging magic and you're learning it at an entirely reasonable pace."

She laughed and managed to stifle most of her frustration. "Well, given how reasonable the rest of my life is, I guess that'll have to be enough." With a shake of her head, she asked, "Should I try again?"

"No. Your brain isn't in the right place for this. We'll do more later."

"Okay." She strode out of the room and the house, muttering curses under her breath at gangsters, nobles, and everything between.

Her steps took her to the closet-sized room where the wingback chair, the basin, and the rack of ebony rods awaited. She chose a stick at random as she hadn't had enough time to determine the organization the inscribed runes indicated, other than merely being numbers presumably recorded in order over time. Her father's image materialized as she slotted it into place, the frozen frame stern and serious, and she pulled it out immediately.

Nope, one parent speaking from beyond death is all I can take right now, thanks. She inserted another and her mother appeared. A moment later, her still form became animated and she smiled at her child.

"Hello, love."

"Hi, Mom."

The apparition tilted her head to the side. "You seem troubled. How can I help?"

The whole experience was weird and she struggled to grasp the idea that they'd left pieces of themselves to share specific information but which were also able to interact with her like she imagined her true parents would have. "Which of the houses should I trust most?"

Her mother's face fell into a frown. "When I created this memory for you, none of them. We sought help when the troubles began and were refused by some, strung along by others, and betrayed by two who pretended an alliance but turned on us. In secret, of course, with smiles on their faces in public." Her opinion of those people came through in her acerbic tone. Cali couldn't remember the woman having been that judgmental in the time they'd shared.

"Who were they?"

A look of uncertainty crossed her face. "Are you sure that is an answer you want? Much has undoubtedly changed since this version of me lived. It might be erroneous information by now."

She shook her head. "Things don't change that quickly and evil is always evil. Please tell me."

The apparition shrugged. "House Terriau was the first to reveal themselves. Fortunately, we were suspicious of them and planted false intelligence. They shared it with our enemies."

"Terriau. Got it. And who else?"

Her mother sighed. "The other was the most wicked cut of all. We trusted them—trusted them all—for generations. But when the moment in which an opportunity to trade loyalty for power arrived, they abandoned us without hesitation."

Her blood pounded in her ears and filled her with cold anger. She realized her fists were clenched only when the ache broke through her other emotions. "Who?"

"House Rivette."

A whooshing noise occupied her head as her thoughts crashed into one another. *House Rivette. We were betrayed by the house that bore, nurtured, and raised Shenni to the lofty heights of Empress.*

CHAPTER SIX

Tanyith had arrived before Barton and held down a corner stool in the dark bar. The space was filled with Russian propaganda posters lit by small spotlights and featured a giant red star that adorned the largest wall. He loved the atmosphere. Even more, he enjoyed the fact that despite its prime location on Decatur, the venue drew almost no one other than locals, especially this late in the evening when they were mostly focused on making fools of themselves on Bourbon Street.

It isn't great for the bar, but it's perfect for me.

The door opened to reveal gray night beyond and a silhouette he recognized instantly. Kendra Barton had initially appeared to be an opponent but somewhere along the line, they'd realized the spark between them wasn't only conflict. While they still had significant differences of opinion, those hadn't yet overwhelmed the feelings they shared. She was dressed in her normal date clothes—black jeans and boots, a form-fitting blue top, and a black leather biker jacket over it. He knew she'd have weapons on her as well, plus the heavy-duty cell phone her job as a detective for the NOPD required.

She slipped onto the chair beside him and leaned in for a kiss. It was more than a greeting but less than an invitation for more. Her short hair had found its natural state, messy but still purposefully so. She wore only a trace of makeup, a little darkening around the eyes and lips. It was rare for her to go all out as the nights when she got a call outside of her alleged working hours were more frequent than not. They'd been to the bar enough that the man serving the spirits knew what they wanted, and a cherry vodka tonic appeared in front of her shortly after she sat.

Her presence pulled a smile from him, as usual. "Did you have a tough day?"

Kendra shrugged. "Same old, same old. There seems to be a lull in the fight between the gangs, though. Only a few isolated incidents here and there."

"Surely that's a good thing?" Tanyith asked.

Her expression somber, she shook her head. "Maybe. Maybe not. If this is the quiet before a storm, that would be bad. And we have no indication at all of what's behind the change. So, naturally, we assume the worst."

"Locally or more?"

"More. The FBI is concerned. The staties are worried. And my folks are here on the sharp end of the stick with no idea of what the hell is going on." Her frustration rose as she spoke, and she finished with a heavy exhale as if to vent the emotions. "But that's hardly worth discussing since we can't do anything about it at the moment." She drained her drink in several large gulps and gestured for a refill. "Is everything okay with you?"

He nodded. "More or less. I'm still looking for damn Aiden Walsh. I'll give the search another month and then let it go."

She laughed and shook her head. "You're such a knight, Tay. You would have fit right in at Arthur's round table." She sighed. "I found some things out. About the Leblancs."

A chill wave swept through him and made his head spin for a moment. It wasn't only the abrupt change of topic, although that was part of it.

It's a police interview tactic. I should be used to it by now.

The detective had reacted very differently to the revelation that Cali's parents had been involved in a secret fight in New Orleans. He'd seen them as good people trying to work against the bad elements but she'd named them vigilantes. Their oppositional views had caused no small amount of stress between them.

Tanyith nodded. "Okay. Let me have it."

"Aside from a couple who were picked up by the police and are serving terms in jail, every one of the people they had posted is either missing or dead."

A strange collection of information had covered a wall in Cali's parents' bunker like the work of a movie serial killer with papers, highlights, and thick string illustrating the web of connections between items. To him, it had appeared to be an effort to get a view of the big picture of crime in the city during the years they spent in New Orleans before they were killed by person or persons unknown.

"It could be coincidence."

She gave him the withering look she dredged up from time to time. "No, it couldn't. Not with the other things we found in there." She was referring to armor, spy gadgets, healing potions, and other items that would be useful either to good people fighting bad ones or to vigilantes.

"There were no weapons," he countered.

"Magicals don't always need them, or so I've been told." Left unsaid was that he was the one who had supplied that information when he described some of the ritual battles he and Cali had been involved in against the Atlantean gang.

Tanyith sighed. "They're dead, Kendra. Why can't you leave this alone?"

She growled with open irritation. "Because history seems to be repeating itself. The next generation is working outside the law, too. And while I respect—truly respect—the fact that Cali, you, and everyone else involved is trying not to drop bodies, it'll happen, and that's a big line to cross."

It had already happened. There had merely been no proof left for the police to find. They hadn't had any other option, but that event would still meet Kendra's criteria of wrong.

And she might be correct. But someone has to do something, right?

And there it was, the line she insisted he had to choose a side of. To obey the rule of law and let the police deal with everything, or fight for justice outside those boundaries. It was a tightrope with a chasm on either side, and she wanted him to jump in one direction or the other.

He shook his head. "So what do you suggest? Until New Orleans gets an AET force, the magical problem will continue to be one you can't get a handle on. You know it, even if you don't want to admit it."

Kendra sighed. "I do. But there's a fairly wide space between self-defense and targeting people without the blessing and the protection of the law. And I'm worried—really worried—that you'll wind up in prison again or worse." Her emotions were raw and as honest as he'd ever seen from her. Unfortunately, he couldn't give her the answer she wanted.

He raised his hands, then let them fall. "We're doing the best we can. If you're able to find a way to resolve things in a better way, it's a win for all of us. Until then, Cali can't stand idly by. Nor can I."

She took a deep breath and abruptly switched gears. "So, let's shove all that in a box for now. I need help with a thing."

"What kind of thing? I'm quite helpful." He added enough playfulness to it to draw a smile.

"Not that kind of thing. I have a lead on a building that might be harboring gang activity. Unfortunately, the word came from an informant of questionable reputation so I can't get a warrant. But I still need to check it out and do a little recon—everything the law will allow."

"And you're asking me for help why?"

"I'm told it has magical protection."

He raised a hand with the palm out. "Hold up, now. Maybe you should give me more information. That sounds very much like you stepping onto the line you mentioned earlier."

Kendra sighed. "I need a drink." She pointed for a refill for both of them and drummed her fingers on the bar for half a minute, lost in thought. Finally, she swiveled on her chair and met his gaze.

"It's like this. I can't stop you and I can't stop Cali. I understand why, even though I don't like it. What I can do, within the bounds of my personal and professional ethics, is to turn my attention more toward the threats you face since they're also threats to the city as a whole. This could be one of those."

He reached for her hand and she let him take it. "Are you sure that's something you're comfortable with?"

She laughed. "If not, you'll be the first to hear."

"Okay, tell me what you know."

"So, with the lull between the Zatoras and the Atlanteans, it's not a stretch to imagine that one or both is planning something. Now, we get word about strangers going in and out of this warehouse in the middle of nowhere. The informant couldn't tell me much more, but it seems a reasonable guess that either one group or the other is bringing people or items in."

"Like soldiers and weapons." He kept the alarm out of his voice, but the idea that the gangs were planning to go for broke against each other scared him deeply. "I can see why you're concerned."

"Right." She nodded. "And I don't want to be fried by a magical defense or whatever on the way in."

"Doesn't the NOPD have magical consultants?"

"Sure. They are easily accessible by those with warrants."

"Gotcha. Of course I'll help. And maybe you can do more searching for the damned enigma I'm chasing afterward."

Kendra laughed. "You know, I could be jealous about how far you're willing to go for your ex-girlfriend. Fortunately for you, I'm aware that you're merely insanely obsessive about everything."

He grinned. "Guilty as charged. So, when do you want to do it?"

"I'm free now."

Tanyith stared at her in surprise, then shrugged. "All right. Let's take a look."

CHAPTER SEVEN

The warehouse was truly in the middle of nowhere, as Kendra had said. Tanyith walked several steps in front of her, his physical and magical senses focused on the three-story rectangular structure ahead of them. It filled half of a block in the industrial park beside an identical structure in the remaining portion.

Signs of life showed around the closest one. A light glowed in some of the dirt-encrusted windows on the top level, a door creaked, and the bright flicker of a lighter indicated that someone had stepped outside for a cigarette.

Their angle of approach left him feeling vulnerable. He would have preferred to go high and cross from rooftop to rooftop. His human companion was one argument against that, and the strong probability of magical wards ready to knock him from the air was another. So instead, he dashed from shadow to shadow as best he could and closed the distance steadily. Kendra's stealth skills were more than adequate, and he felt more than sensed her presence behind him.

An instant before he stepped onto the sidewalk that bounded the building, alarm surged through him and he froze and raised an arm to halt his partner. Cautiously, he focused his attention on the ten feet in front of him. The magical wards were exceedingly clever and would have been very easy to overlook if he hadn't already been warned about their probable presence. He crouched to present a smaller profile as he traced the threads. What he found shocked him, and he leaned closer to whisper to Kendra, who had shuffled into place beside him.

"These are tricky bastards, whoever they are. There's no way I would have located the traps normally. The magical wards are extremely low power because they're only triggers."

He pointed to a nearby bush, which appeared at first glance to be an innocuous part of a formerly vibrant landscaping effort. Only by staring at it for several seconds with the knowledge that something had to be there had he been able to discern it. A claymore mine faced the street, ready to unleash its payload of ball bearings to shred anyone who tripped the ward. "They're not kidding around."

"Holy hell." Her breath hitched. "That's serious overkill."

Tanyith nodded. "I would say it's more likely to be a Zatora location, given the access to military gear and if you hadn't mentioned the sightings of magicals. Even though they clearly have some magic support, I can't imagine they have an abundance of it."

"But they could import more, right?"

For a moment, he considered the question in silence, then shook his head. "I don't think they'd be able to find many individuals willing to fight other magicals on their behalf, no matter how much they were paid. There are less conflicted paths to wealth for people with magic."

She snorted softly. "You mean like endless private investigative work for no pay?"

"Shut it. I need to concentrate here." He stretched his magic forward in search of the weakest areas in the ward. It came as no surprise to find those he was familiar with and so expected, but he also took time to hunt for other defensive magics. What he discovered made him even more concerned. "It's completely wrapped by a mixture of physical and magical defenses. It was a good call not to try to do this yourself."

"Are we able to get through it?"

"Yeah. I can definitely stop us from getting killed by the wards, but I'm not positive I can avoid being noticed by the people and killed by them instead. My attention will have to be on the magic. Is it worth it?"

Kendra gestured at the building. "What do you think? What do they need to ward so heavily? It has to be more than people, right?"

Tanyith nodded. "I would say so, especially given the hardware. All right, then. Step where I step and stay directly behind me. If I stop, you stop." His favorite mode of escape was regrettably off the table as going airborne would mean leaving her behind.

Which means I have to get this right on the first try. Okay, Tay, don't screw it up.

The path that threaded through the wards showed no signs of being trampled from use and offered no indication that it was any different than the grass and dirt around it.

They thought of everything. Whoever they are. He traveled it one cautious step at a time, although he tried to go fast enough that random chance wouldn't get them caught. At the same time, he needed to move slowly enough that if another trap awaited them that he hadn't seen, he might have a chance to sense it before it blew up in his face.

No other threats emerged, fortunately, and they arrived at a side entrance without further incident. He was surprised when the knob turned, then laughed and whispered, "It figures. With all that protection, there's no bloody need to lock up." Two cigarette butts on the ground provided an additional explanation as to why it might be unlocked and emphasized the need for them to hurry.

"Are we safe from magic problems?" Kendra asked. He cracked the door open and pushed his power forward but identified no wards beyond.

"I don't see anything obvious."

She slipped past him. "Okay, now you follow me." She mimed a look of surprise. "I think I heard a shout in there like someone was hurt. Didn't you?" She opened the door only far enough to slide through and he followed but paused long enough to ensure that its return to closure was silent.

The inside resembled every storage warehouse he'd ever been in, with a lofty ceiling above and vast floor space to stack pallets and crates and whatever else required a temporary home. The items there were in large wooden boxes, cheaply made and unmarked. Each crate measured about three feet high by four long and was neither particularly wide nor particularly shallow. They were stacked two-high in places and three-high in others, with a smattering of single ones here and there. They crawled behind one of these and peered over it toward the center.

Red spray paint demarcated a circular area on the floor, a wavering line about six feet in diameter. Another six feet in each direction was bare, with boxes arranged more or less at random beyond that distance.

"It's not exactly a logistical success," he whispered,

Kenda nodded and pointed at the same moment that he heard laughter. Across the warehouse, two men approached from a rough corridor between towers of crates. Their long heavy locks indicated that they were almost certainly Atlantean, but he didn't recognize them from his time with the gang. Their words were still too soft to make out and remained that way until they reached the red circle.

One stood and faced the middle while the other watched him with a mocking expression and said, "Are you sure you're up to it?"

"Bite me, loser. This isn't anything at all. It's easy."

"Yeah, that's why you almost collapsed last time."

The other man growled belligerently. "Shut up. That was the rum you convinced me to drink." Laughter was the only reply, and he turned to the center again, which gave them a perfect look at his face as he raised his hands and spoke arcane words. A small hole appeared about five feet off the floor, directly in the middle of the ring, and began to extend from there. By the time it completed the expansion, it reached the cement below and ten feet toward the ceiling.

"It's a portal," Tanyith whispered. "And that looks like another warehouse on the other side." Figures stepped through the rift in space and dragged carts with more crates on them, all identical to those already present. He shook his head. "Okay, my guess is that they're bringing stuff from New Atlantis. We always knew the local gang had a hookup. I suppose this is it."

Kendra frowned. "Then why the secrecy? And why didn't we know about it?"

He shrugged. "Maybe there are competing elements within the gang? That wouldn't be unheard of. And it would work to our advantage."

"I suppose there could be. I think the wards are enough to request surveillance, which should give us access to whatever information we need for a warrant."

She drifted past him toward the door, but when he moved to follow, another arrival from the portal caught his attention. He recognized the woman he'd seen at the Privateer Pub in New Atlantis. Her freckles and thin blonde hair were impossible to miss.

If she's here, this is a Malniet warehouse. Which means they're planning something for the city again and I need to get the hell out of here before they see me.

Tanyith hurried past Kendra and led the way through the wards without detection. When they were clear, they walked the couple of blocks to her car in silence. He climbed in the passenger side of the Charger, while she took the driver's seat and eased the vehicle onto the road.

After several minutes without conversation, she asked, "Is everything okay? Are you good?"

He shook his head. "No. Those weren't the Zatoras or the local Atlanteans. I recognized one of them at the end.

They're from New Atlantis and are the ones who brought the Kraken and who later attacked the city."

She growled and pressed on the accelerator to pass a Honda driven somewhat erratically. "Exactly what we need —another gang in town. The feds will love this."

"No. You can't tell them. They're the ones who have me on the hook, and I'm sure they know about you too. You need to keep this quiet until I find a way to free myself from them or they won't stop until they've killed us both— plus Sienna and maybe Cali."

"Damn it." Her words were low but clearly heartfelt. "Are there no other options? How about we arrest them all?"

He snorted. "What's the extradition law like with New Atlantis? Are your local jails warded against portals? And you have anti-magic emitters, do you?"

Kendra sighed and repeated more softly, "Damn it. No, of course not." With a shake of her head, she added, "You know this is exactly what I was talking about. Now I'm in the same damned situation."

"You could walk away."

"Yeah, right. No, they're a threat and if we can't deal with them publicly, we need to do what we can to stop them privately. And if you say a single word to me about lines or whatever, you don't get to come home with me."

Tanyith spent the rest of the drive in silence while his mind considered the situation from every angle in search of the weakness he was sure was there. By the time the engine switched off, he had come no closer to it than when he'd started but remained certain it was there for the finding.

CHAPTER EIGHT

C ali stood on a bench so she would be eye to eye with the hulking Kilomea who had insulted her. He was new to the bar and deep in his cups, and she knew the routine well. It was a test and she was up to it. She stared into the dark-black orbs in his oversized face and growled a challenge.

"Do you care to say that again, Sasquatch?"

He chuckled and his heavy voice bounced off the walls closest to him at the rear of the tavern's common room while the surrounding conversations halted. He'd chosen the back corner for his drinking and unlike most of his kind she'd seen in the Drunken Dragons, he had come alone. They most often arrived in groups, which provided an element of control to limit the most aggressive ones. This Kilomea, though, wasn't limiting anything.

"I said, get me another drink, tiny wench, and do it right this second."

The test was to see if she was someone to be respected

or not. While she tended toward the "Respect until proven otherwise" end of the spectrum when meeting people, his species were far more on the "No respect until proven otherwise" end of the continuum. In any case, it was a moment of liveliness in a thus-far boring Thursday night. She'd come back from New Atlantis the day before in time for her shift and that had been equally unexciting.

Either the bar's slow or I'm less patient. I'm sure it's the bar. I'm perfect. She snorted at herself and said, "You're new here so I'll let that one slide. But if you don't rephrase it, you'll have the embarrassing experience of being thrown out of here on your face."

He laughed deeply and looked past her. "By the dwarf behind the bar? I hear he doesn't bring that ax down for anything. And he's even smaller than you."

Cali shook her head. *Ticking me off is one thing but getting Zeb mad is a bad, bad idea.* She'd never seen her boss truly angry but imagined it would be a rough experience for whoever inspired it.

"Nah. I don't need help to take the trash out. The bigger it is, the farther it flies when I throw it." She kept her gaze locked on his and a slow smile emerged on his face.

"All right then. Another drink, please. But you're still tiny."

She laughed. "Only compared to some, big guy." She jumped down and headed to the bar, and the normal sounds of discussion and merriment resumed. When she reached the counter, she shook her head at Zeb. "Some people, am I right?"

He grinned. "Well handled, as always. Hopefully, he'll

find friends before he gets so drunk you do have to throw him out of here." It wasn't really a worry. The dwarf was very good at monitoring his patrons and would slow or stop their intake as required to avoid problems. Sometimes, they had to give out a free meal of the day's stew and bread, but watching out for his customers—even when they didn't want to be watched out for—was a sacred part of the job for him. She admired both his dedication and his single-mindedness about it.

I wish I could be single-minded about anything, these days. Her brain was a constant flutter of issues and worries. It was one of the reasons she wouldn't let her shifts at the tavern slide any more than necessary. She needed relief from her thoughts and was able to easily lose herself in the work when it was busy.

"I'm mostly sure I can juice my muscles enough to do it but I might wind up injured. He's kind of big."

Zeb nodded. "And it's better to be careful with that. I've seen people push beyond their limits with magic. It's not pretty."

"Well, then, I certainly can't do that because I'm so very pretty." She laughed. "Who would want to mess up this?" She gestured at herself and the oh-so-fashionable black jeans and concert t-shirt she wore and shook her head.

I never wanted to be a model, anyway. I like food.

Any answer was forestalled by a series of shouts from behind her. Cali rolled her eyes and went to defuse whatever argument had broken out.

Near the end of her shift, when only a few stragglers remained and with less than ten minutes before it was time to lock the entrance, the calm familiarity of the evening was shattered. The front door banged violently to slam against the wall, which made everyone look in that direction. A man in a hoodie and jeans walked in, followed by an attractive woman in a suit.

Cali set her tray down and loosened her hold on her magic to make sure it was ready for instant recall. Another member of the Atlantean gang entered and closed the door quietly.

Her boss immediately took action. "Everyone out. Go now." The authority in his voice galvanized the patrons into compliance and a few moments later, the three Atlanteans were the only ones present besides her, Zeb, and Fyre. The Draksa was behind the bar, and while she couldn't see him, the sense of calm alertness that flowed over their mental connection reassured her that he was as ready as she was to deal with anything that might happen.

The proprietor turned to Danna Cudon and the men with her and offered a mild rebuke. "Try not to slam the door, please. It alarms the customers."

She nodded with a smile that suggested that had been her intent. "Noted, dwarf."

He returned the gesture. "Thank you, Atlantean. Manners never hurt. We are living in a society here, last I checked."

The woman laughed. Cali always wondered how the laugh could sound so friendly when Cudon herself was so...not. "Ah, but there are civilized societies and ones that are less so, aren't there? In any case, I didn't come here to trade clever banter with you." She swiveled to face the young woman. "No, my purpose here is with this one. Greetings, Matriarch."

Her smile in response was thin and not at all friendly. "Lovely to see you as always, Ms. Cudon. Dare I hope that you've decided to surrender—or even better, to offer to settle this one on one between us?"

Her visitor raised an eyebrow in amusement. "You have no idea how much I would relish that opportunity, Caliste. But no, such things are not to be. The next battle will be five on five, tomorrow night at nine at this location." She gestured abruptly and one of the men who'd accompanied her placed an envelope on the bar.

"Another factory? Because that worked out really well for you, I thought."

The smug look didn't leave the Atlantean's face but it stood out more as the rest of her expression became harder. "No, not another factory. I think you'll enjoy it, though." She turned and moved to the door. One of her people preceded her and the other followed, walking backward to keep her enemies in sight.

Once they were gone, Zeb shook his head with a sigh.

"Idiots. They had no reason to bring this inside my tavern. Now, I'm even more irritated with them."

She looked at the dwarf—who appeared no different than he had at any other moment in the evening—and laughed. "Yeah, you sure seem upset."

"I'll join you for this one."

"Come again?" Her humor fled in an instant.

"You heard me. I'm in. It's time to teach these bozos they can't mess with us in our place."

Cali considered it and liked it more with each passing moment. "Okay, I love that idea. I think we'll shove it in their face a little more and go four-on-five. I'm sure that got under their skin last time." She grinned. "Will you bring Valerie?"

Zeb nodded. "I might not use her, but she'll definitely come along."

"They won't expect it, that's for sure. Good. Next time, I might have to take Sensei Ikehara up on his offer—which means I need to find something that will help him defend against magic, at least. Ideally, magic weapons, although I'm not sure there's any Oriceran in his background so that probably wouldn't work out."

Her boss shrugged. "I've never known a non-magical who was able to use magic weapons. But you might ask Nylotte. If there's anyone who knows more about that than I do, it's her."

She nodded. "I'll add that to the list I need to bug her about."

The dagger, learning lightning, the sword, and now, something magical to preserve Ikehara. She'll get tired of dealing with me, at this rate.

"So, what's the plan?" he asked after a moment.

"Do you think we need one?"

He laughed. "No, I don't, at that. So, we simply arrive on time and be ready to rumble?"

"Let's meet at the bunker an hour before and go together from there. I'll let Tanyith know."

Zeb turned to look at the Draksa behind the bar. "Is that good for you, Fyre?" A snort of affirmation followed, which drew a laugh from them both. "All right then. Tomorrow will be a real learning experience for these jerks."

CHAPTER NINE

Cali had practiced with sword and dagger against every weapon present in the dojo and mostly held her own. She was fairly sure, though, that Ikehara had gone easy on her. She slashed from the outside in with the bamboo sword, aimed at the side of his head, and shuffled forward to stab with the practice knife in her off-hand.

The grin that appeared a moment before he countered made it clear that she'd overstepped. He spun the bo staff in his hands to block both weapons, then snaked it out and slapped it against her wrist. She dropped the dagger with a yelp and darted away as the end of his stick sought her head. Hastily, she dropped into a crouch and blocked the next downward strike with her sword, then guided the staff out of the way with it. As she paused to swing it in again, her foe dropped, spun, and cut her legs out from under her with his heel.

She landed on her back, and it was only a second before his weapon was at her throat. Cali moaned, "I yield," and

Ikehara lowered himself beside her as she rose to a seated position.

"What did you do wrong?"

"I agreed to become your student." She sighed and when he laughed, she shook her head. "Honestly, I'm not sure. I thought I had you once I pushed the staff outward."

He nodded. "But you had to generate the swing in the other direction, which gave me time. Is there a way to use your magic to push the staff away or to propel your sword?"

"Perhaps, if I had the gift of telekinesis. But that's one I can't seem to master. So…maybe a force blast to block with. I could probably do that."

"Good. You're learning fast with the sword and dagger combination. In a few more months, you'll be as proficient with them as you are with the sticks."

"If only I had a few more months." She added nothing further, reluctant to burden him, but of course, he refused to simply let her statement lie.

"Why don't you?"

Cali shrugged. "Things are moving faster and it looks more and more like the only way to get ahead of the curve is to make them go faster still."

He nodded. "That is appropriate for an Aikido practitioner. Use your enemy's momentum against them."

"That's enemies, plural. Which makes it a little more difficult since they're not all going in the same direction."

"You'll merely have to be more agile."

"I feel like an elephant among gazelles, Sensei."

Ikehara laughed loudly and clapped his hands. "A clear sign that you are resistant to moving with the speed you need to." He tapped a forefinger gently on her forehead, a gesture he had used often during their early training sessions. "The problem is not in your body. It is in your mind. You are a cheetah. Act like one."

"Right. Easy-peasy."

"If you let it be, it will be." That was another one of his phrases she simultaneously loved and hated. "Now, what also will be is the group class. Prepare."

After the session with the other students, Ikehara had pulled her aside and recommended she spend the afternoon working on her mind rather than her body. She hadn't mentioned the fight that night but she imagined he'd sensed it somehow. Or maybe it was coincidence. Either way, it was a good idea. She'd meditated while she lay in bed, while she stretched and swayed through basic tai chi forms, and while she showered and prepared for what was to come.

Now, arriving at her parents' bunker before the others, she was in a contemplative mood. Fyre moved to the lockers and lay near them, engaged in his pre-fight ritual— extreme relaxation. She snorted.

Pre-fight, pre-sleep, pre-walk, pre-whatever. That is one creature who knows how to chill.

Cali looked at the items on the other wall and the strings that connected them and wondered what her parents had been up to. Tanyith had shared Barton's discovery that the people pinned there were all bad and were missing or dead. He hadn't mentioned anything more, but it was an easy jump to assume the detective wasn't thrilled about the discovery. She hoped it wouldn't be a big issue between them.

There was no way on Earth or Oriceran that she would judge her parents' actions, whatever they were, as anything other than right and necessary, though. She might not understand the why of it all, but she held no doubts about the correctness of their intentions.

She was dying to know what treasure the dagger referenced but had accepted Nylotte's advice to wait and let her investigate it first. That was another thing she didn't understand. Why was the Drow so willing to help her? Of course, at this moment in her life, she was willing to take what was offered. If she survived, she would find a way to repay every favor with interest. If not, she'd trust that Zeb and Tanyith would take care of it for her. Part of her wanted to include Fyre in that group, but she was certain that she and her Draksa life partner wouldn't survive for long without each other.

It wasn't a thought she wanted to focus on so she pulled the uniform out and slipped into it, using the ritual to calm her mind as she always did. While she changed from her shorts into the black trousers, she put away the worries about New Atlantis. They were for after she took the outfit off again. The tight ebony tunic that replaced her t-shirt banished thoughts about the Zatoras and whatever they were up to. This night was only about the Atlantean gang. As she fastened the jacket, she locked away the bigger concerns with them. The ongoing rituals and their actions in the city were irrelevant. The only thing that mattered was defeating the five opponents they'd bring to the fight.

The next step was to check to make sure her potions were in place, even though she'd put them there herself after the previous occasion—two of each on either side of her body in thigh pouches. Her heavy belt from New Atlantis went over everything, along with the glass spheres that held the sharp crystals that had proven so useful before. Invel had been willing but not exactly happy to supply more. She felt the same about using them—willing but reluctantly so.

But I will do what I need to do. She glanced at the wall again, filled with papers and photos and string. *Exactly like they did.*

Fyre sensed the portal an instant before she did, raised his head, and looked expectantly at the center of the room. She turned as the rift solidified to reveal the basement of the Drunken Dragons Tavern on the other side behind her friends. Tanyith and Zeb walked through, and the magical passage dwindled and faded. She nodded, and they returned the gesture.

Zeb looked around and chuckled. "I love what you've done to the place—which is to say absolutely nothing."

That drew a laugh from Tanyith and eventually from her as well. Leave it to him to find something to jab her about, no matter when or where they happened to be.

"I've been busy," she countered. "My boss is a hard taskmaster." The man smothered a smile and headed to the lockers.

The dwarf put his hands on his hips. She'd never seen the clothes he wore now, an all-black ensemble that included heavy boots and trousers, a thick shirt, and a vest over it. The latter item seemed extra bulky, and she wondered what might be hidden under or inside it. He also wore wide bracers that she instantly recognized as magical weapons similar to her sticks, and the broad handle of his battle-ax Valerie was visible over one shoulder. "I'll have you know that you work only half as hard as Janice does these days."

Cali scowled. "That's low. Really low. Think for a minute what a shambles the Dragons would be without me. Like, a literal shambles. You'd have to come out from behind the bar constantly to break altercations up, and you'd hate that." She shook her head. "Janice. Please."

He laughed. "Fair enough. But that doesn't make this place any more attended to."

"Shut up or I'll attend to you."

Fyre snorted, and Zeb grinned. He clapped his hands slowly. "Good one. I feel properly threatened now."

She sighed but couldn't keep her smile hidden. "Shut it. You're supposed to be on my side."

"And I am, always. That means I'm not allowed to lie to you."

Her retort was interrupted when Tanyith asked, "So, is there any special plan for tonight?"

Cali turned to where he'd already changed into the trousers and tunic and now buttoned the jacket. Zeb stepped forward to complete the small circle of people around the recumbent Draksa, who seemed unconcerned with either their positioning or conversation. She sensed only a sleepy confidence from him, which she tried to pull into her mind.

"If only I could be more like you, buddy," she sent to

him, and a thread of mirth joined the other feelings that coursed between them.

"She's kind of light on strategy," the dwarf quipped, "from what I've seen."

With a sigh, she replied, "Shut it. We can't decide on a strategy until we see the venue. But ultimately, it's the same. Choose an opponent, overcome them however we need to, and move on to help the others."

"Are you not worried anymore about using magic right off the bat?" Tanyith asked.

She shook her head. "Nah. I think I was wrong to care about that. Or maybe it made sense early on when we still had tricks to reveal but not so much now that we all know each other so well. Anyway, do what you feel you need to do." She turned to her boss. "You're the surprise of the day. Is there anything we need to know?"

He shrugged. "I can take on the extra one if needed. I'm fairly good at fighting multiples and have considerable experience in that arena. Plus, out of all of us, I've almost definitely faced the largest number of different types of magic. You and Fyre should probably work as a team as much as possible, and Tanyith and I will try to do the same."

Cali nodded. "Assuming the battleground allows us to. I looked on the Internet and found some floor plans, but the abandoned hospital is essentially what you'd expect it to be— a maze of rooms and hallways, all of which are in danger of imminent collapse. I wouldn't be shocked to find sections that already have. On the plus side, the blasted giant crab won't fit there. And I can't imagine there will be many spectators."

Tanyith looked thoughtful. "Are traps allowed within the rules?"

"Probably not ones set in advance but we should keep our eyes open. They've proven any number of times that following the letter of the law is not something that concerns them overly much."

"It's a good arrangement for us." Zeb sounded happy. "We're all adept at close-quarters battle. This will take away their big magical advantages like long-range attacks and mutated creatures."

"Big mutated creatures," she clarified. "They could have smaller ones. There have been Draksa the last couple of times."

"Fair enough." The dwarf didn't sound concerned about the possibility. "But it still plays to our strengths."

"Which makes you wonder why they chose it, doesn't it?" Tanyith asked suspiciously. "They have to be aware of that, too."

She considered his question, which made sense and was something they needed to keep in mind. "They didn't know about Zeb. Perhaps they thought this would be effective against you and I and Fyre? It definitely cuts out the aerial advantage."

"I don't know." The man sounded skeptical. "Maybe there's another reason, like whoever they bring are better in this environment, too."

Cali nodded. "And that's why we can't have nice things like strategy. So, how about we simply get there and get this over with?"

They'd be a little early but she wasn't worried about that. She wished absently that she hadn't left her new dagger with Nylotte but she'd decided the knowledge on it was too important to risk. Any lead to her parents was more valuable than gold at the moment.

Tanyith finished securing his jacket and summoned the first of the three portals they'd use to reach the location. "You're right. Enough talking. Let's do it."

CHAPTER TEN

A few moments later, Cali was the first to step out of the portal onto the grounds of the abandoned hospital. The lower area where the emergency room had been had become a small lake full of unhealthy looking water. Ahead was a glassed-in lobby entrance, and the metal doors inside stood open. She sniffed the air and caught the odors of mildew and mold and rotting vegetation. "Eww."

Fyre sneezed, a clear signal of his agreement.

Zeb's expression evidenced his disgust. "There are no sounds—no birds or insects or anything. This is not a place for living beings."

Tanyith strode ahead but stopped at the entrance and gestured expansively for her to precede him. She rolled her eyes. "Always the gentleman, especially when it involves heading into danger."

He gave her a small smile. "You know it."

His nerves were showing. She hoped she did a better job of hiding hers, but they were there and tried to convince her to leave rather than cross the threshold into the facility. Cali forced herself through the doorway and into the darkness beyond. A glowing orb was positioned down the hallway to the left, so she headed in that direction and the others followed. Fyre transmitted a combination of wariness and comfort, which set her mind at ease.

I guess I don't need to worry about him being hampered by the venue if he's not worried about it.

The lamps led them along a labyrinthine path and eventually down a wide staircase. A short distance beyond that was a room that spilled light into the corridor from the doorway on the right-hand wall. She stopped and turned to the others.

"This is your last chance to back out." Tanyith shook his head and Zeb merely laughed. She turned, her spirits buoyed, and strode into the room with her magic pressed demandingly against her ability to restrain it.

She'd expected a crowd and perhaps a nightmarish creature awaiting them. Instead, only six people were present in what had clearly once been a cafeteria. One was Danna Cudon, dressed as ever in a suit and tie. She looked worn in the shadows thrown by the orbs. The other five were indistinguishable from each other. They seemed like statues in the familiar black crab-shell armor with full helmets to hide their features. By their size, she could determine that they weren't Kilomea, dwarves, or gnomes, but that was about all she could decisively commit to.

Tanyith muttered behind her, and Zeb responded with something she didn't hear. Her attention was focused on the Atlantean leader, who stepped forward at their arrival.

Cudon wore the familiar smirk but it also seemed worn and drained.

"Maybe she's tired of losing," Cali sent to Fyre and received a touch of mirth in return. The other woman's voice was less triumphant than usual, as well.

"Caliste Leblanc, do you wish to forfeit?"

Cali shook her head. "No, but you certainly could. You started this and you could end it right now. Your people don't have to risk their lives over this stupid ritual."

The gang second in command shrugged. "Those are meaningless concerns. The champions welcome the fight as a way to prove themselves. If they fail, they were never worthy, to begin with." She expected to see some kind of reaction from the others, but they remained motionless. "It is unlikely all your friends will survive the day, even if you manage to emerge victorious. Perhaps you'd like time to say your goodbyes?"

"Shut it, wench. Let's do this." Anger spiked within her and for a moment, she wondered what the consequences would be of setting the woman ablaze. Fyre's continued confidence helped her steady herself.

"Very well. In one minute, the combat begins." Without any other indication, the five statues blurred into motion, separated, and raced from the room through several exits. "It ends, as always, with the incapacitation or death of the opposing force. I will be here, awaiting the return of your bodies when you have failed."

She grinned. "Are you sure you don't want to make it six on four, hmm? Or are you still hiding behind the whole 'I'm not allowed' excuse? Who holds your puppet strings, anyway?"

With a dismissive wave, the woman moved to a darkened corner of the room and vaulted onto a table where she sat cross-legged and closed her eyes.

Cali had no doubt that she was nonetheless keenly aware of them and ready to defend herself if need be. She turned to her teammates.

Zeb said, "They'll rely on darkness but my people come from underground and I can see better than most. Tanyith and I will be fine."

"As can I, and as will we," Fyre replied. He sounded eager to get into the battle, and she wondered if it was her emotions rolling onto him or if his were influencing her desire for a fight. *Either way, the result's the same.*

She willed her bracelets to transform into sticks and nodded. "All right, then. Let's go clean up." She tapped her earpiece to turn it on and Tanyith and Zeb did the same. "Remember, no dying. I don't have that many friends and I don't want to lose you."

She turned and headed to the door where two of their enemies had vanished a few moments before, Fyre at her side.

Tanyith trailed behind Zeb and felt entirely uncomfortable in the dark environment which left him only able to detect obstacles in the corridor when he bumped into them. He hadn't realized how much the orbs had pushed away the ominous sense of blindness until they'd moved beyond the dim lights.

"Maybe we should create some light of our own?" he whispered.

Zeb replied at the same volume. "We'd make ourselves easy targets if we did that." The comm system allowed them to speak softly enough that their words wouldn't reveal them to their enemies.

"Not if they're able to see in the dark already."

The dwarf paused as if to think it over. Finally, he said, "It's a fair point. But we have to assume there are limitations on that ability. Using a light would make us too visible. That's doubtless what they expect us to do, so we shouldn't do it."

He wanted to argue but couldn't fault the summary of the tactical situation. In the larger game, revealing themselves would be bad despite how much better it would make him feel at the moment. He muttered, "Fine, but I'll hide behind you."

His partner chuckled. "Best of luck with that, tall person." He hissed softly and stopped. "There's an intersection ahead. It looks like a nice position for an ambush with doors on the other side of it from us. It might be impassable but I can't tell."

"What's the plan?"

"I'll run through and stop at the doors. If they attack me, you can jump into the fight."

Tanyith frowned. "Are you sure that's a good idea?"

The dwarf's voice carried a certainty he envied. "Yep. The chances are they'll aim high if they're waiting and if they don't, my axes will stop whatever they throw."

"Even magic?"

"Yep."

"Well. Okay then." He drew his Sai with a twirl and wished they were magical. *Maybe there will be something in the treasure vault or whatever it is that Cali's parents left her the clue about.* He focused his mind, brought his magic to a ready state, and exhaled to set his nerves. "I'm good to go."

Zeb barreled through the intersection, invisible in the darkness. No attack came and after a moment, he said. "The door's jammed. It looks like we have to turn back."

Tanyith sighed. "Awesome. Something tells me this will suck."

As she crept along the corridor behind Fyre, Cali had to grin at Tanyith's complaints in her earpiece. "Tay says this will suck," she sent to the Draksa and he returned a sense of amusement to her across their mental connection. Her words wouldn't reach them unless she toggled her microphone, but she'd asked the others to leave theirs active so she'd know what was going on.

Unexpectedly, he said, "I wish I could share my eyesight with you for this."

She frowned. "Is that even possible?"

"I don't know. But it would be helpful."

Cali chuckled. "You might as well wish for me to be able to change into a Draksa."

He chuffed a laugh. "That would be very useful. You should work on that."

"It's exactly what I need. Curse of the Were-Draksa. No thanks."

"Corner ahead," he hissed and she immediately stopped.

They'd agreed he would be the scout, so she waited while he moved ahead. "Clear," he said a moment later.

She stepped forward to follow him again, sensed the space widening around her, and asked, "What do you see?"

"Big room. Center desk area. Smaller rooms on the outside."

"It sounds like an intensive care setup or specialized ward or something. And it sounds dangerous. Can you see them if they're in one of the side rooms?"

His reply sounded irritated. "No. I'm not able to see through walls any more than you are."

"Well, what good are you, then?" She snorted softly in playful mockery.

The quality of his voice changed as the volume dropped. "Good enough to know there's at least one hiding in the back."

While she knew it wasn't wise, she couldn't help herself. The dread the darkness invoked had begun to fill her and she had to act against it. With a shout, she channeled her magic through her sticks, a skill she'd fought hard to master after Nylotte gave her the key to it. A small, controlled ball of flame erupted from the left one and made its way slowly across the room. Shadows skittered in all directions and she located the enemy Fyre had identified. Immediately, she launched a force blast through the other stick and the hospital bed near him lurched up and into the wall as he dodged.

Cali raced ahead and only the sudden motion out of the corner of her eye gave her the chance to dodge the line of shadow that sliced through where her head had just been. Neither of them had seen the other enemy, who had waited for her to reveal herself. Fyre veered in that direction as she dove behind the central desk to avoid the second beam of coherent darkness. She tapped her earpiece and said, "We have two here."

"None here yet," Zeb replied. While his vision was better than average, he still had difficulty making out all the shapes that appeared in his sight. Some were familiar like the wheelchairs and mobile cabinets he carefully avoided. Tanyith had gotten smart and put a hand on his shoulder after he'd banged into one of the latter—once he'd finished cursing about it.

But he wasn't able to recognize others at all such as the large cylindrical machines that resembled some kind of science fiction movie pods in the rooms they passed.

It's probably good the power's not on. Who knows what kinds of trouble these idiots might be able to cause if it was. He grew more antsy with each passing moment that didn't reveal a foe because that was one more moment in which a trap could be set for them.

He had no warning that the floor would collapse beneath him, but the way no debris fell told him instantly it was because he'd stepped onto an illusion. He curled and protected his head as he landed, then uncoiled and darted to his feet in time to identify the glow of magic from three places in the room.

"I have the other three," he told Cali through the comm-link and raised his axes to deal with the imminent ambush.

CHAPTER ELEVEN

The dwarf skittered to the left to avoid the blast from the first enemy to respond. A crackling beam of lightning struck a wooden cabinet full of fabric and set it ablaze. He caught the second and third beams on his axes, which drew the magic in and absorbed the power easily. His movements calm and deliberate, he continued to circle to put the nearest adversary in the way of the others before he attacked, glad to be done with the stalking portion of the challenge.

He pointed the axes as he ran and returned the lightning to his foe. It wreathed him in blue and yellow energy that sparked and dissipated much more quickly than expected. The outline of the armor pieces glowed brightly before they faded to darkness again. He growled.

"They have magic absorption of some kind in their armor," he told his teammates. *Which is fine by me.*

Zeb vaulted upward to avoid another bolt of electricity that was aimed too low—a common mistake that those who fought dwarves for the first time often made—and brought both axes in from the sides. They swung on a downward angle, aimed at the gap in the armor between helmet and shoulder. His adversary managed to spin away and draw a sword before he landed, which required him to dive forward to evade the slice the man dispatched a second later.

His roll carried him to the next man, and he caught that one's sword on crossed axes above his head, mere inches before the blade would have connected. He lashed out with a heavy boot and found his foe's armored knee but couldn't follow up on the man's loss of balance as the first one struck from behind.

The dwarf made his own pirouette, doubtless more agile than the armored man or woman expected, and delivered a wicked backhand. The ax caught the plate that covered his opponent's thigh, which cracked with a loud snap. He fired lightning into the newly created seam and the piece shattered. Once again, he was forced to evade when the second assailant launched another onslaught.

A heavy crash sounded and he dashed sideways to avoid it. He turned to where Tanyith battled the third and realized that the sound had apparently been his leap from the upper floor.

He has more bravery than sense, that one. He grinned at the improved odds and darted in the direction of the nearest foe.

The second line of shadow seared through the desk Cali hid behind like it was nothing more than paper. She'd had the sense to stay low, which was all that kept her head attached to her body. The emotions she associated with Fyre being in combat flowed to her, and she decided she could safely emerge as he'd engaged her attacker. She used a low-power force blast to launch up and over the counter and landed in a run toward where she'd seen the first enemy.

He darted out from cover and launched lightning at her. She threw her left-hand stick at his head and summoned a force shield in a single motion to catch the attack. Her foe batted the stick aside with a hastily drawn sword and knocked it into the small room he'd occupied before he stepped out to swing the weapon at her.

She circled her remaining stick from high to low, arrested his blade, and shoved it away. The move opened his ribs, and she was halfway through delivering a reflexive kick before her brain shouted that he wore armor and she was being stupid. Instead, she planted the leg, used it to jump away from him, and barely avoided his backhand swipe.

"Damn it," Cali muttered and pointed her stick. She channeled fire into the weapon again and this time, launched a wide cone of flame at her opponent. It coated him, covered him, and vanished when the outlines of his armor glowed. "Double damn."

Zeb had just told her that and she'd already forgotten the warning in the heat of the moment. *Get your head in the fight, Cali.*

While she couldn't spare a glance to see how Fyre was doing, she trusted he was holding his own. The dance wouldn't last, though, for either of them. There wasn't enough room for proper evasion, and they'd be caught off balance eventually. The only way out was through. She pumped magic into her muscles to increase her speed, yelled, "*Aspida,*" to activate her shield charm, and surged toward the figure in front of her.

Tanyith had planned his leap to fell the armored challenger, but the bastard had moved at the right moment to avoid the attack. Still, he'd managed to stab him in the armor plates that covered both shoulders, and the one on the right had allowed his blade through. His opponent now favored that arm but seemed adequately adept at wielding his sword one-handed.

There's not much chance to hit the shoulder with magic, so I guess it's melee. Too bad Fyre's not here. Claws from above would be perfect right now.

He deflected the descending sword with his Sai and locked the weapon with a deft twist, which opened his foe to an attack. Lacking a better idea, he thrust forward and kicked with both heels, and his heavy boots smacked the chest plate. His enemy was forced back as Tanyith landed on his back and immediately rolled to his feet.

A crack showed in the armor he'd struck, and an idea came to him. He lunged, stabbed his blade into the fracture, and accepted a strike on the head from the pommel of his foe's sword as he was suddenly inside its effective range. With the blade planted securely, he darted away and raised both hands to deliver electricity into it.

His foe's armor bled some of it off but the vulnerability

allowed the rest to penetrate and the figure staggered and fell. He rushed forward in a fury, unable to control his anger, and yanked the helmet off his adversary to reveal a woman's face contorted in agony. In his rage, he barely registered that he'd been wrong about his opponent's gender. He put one hand on the dagger, ready to release a second charge into the weapon to end her.

A small voice tried to caution him but he could barely hear it through the raging blood that pounded in his ears.

Zeb's words broke through the interference. "Tanyith, there's another one. Get back in the fight—now." He shook his head, stood, and turned in time to be struck by a force bolt and hurled across the room. Thankfully, he managed to raise a force shield to absorb most of the impact with the wall that stopped his flight before he staggered forward to find the one who'd hit him.

Fyre didn't fare well against the armored opponent. His breath weapon was unable to get past whatever magical absorption his foe used, his claws had been insufficient to pierce the armor plates on the couple of times he'd connected, and the confined space hindered his ability to put his natural agility into use. Basically, he merely kept his enemy busy, which was not a situation he enjoyed at all.

The only positive part was that his adversary was similarly unable to manage a decisive strike against him. His clumsy swings—he could sense it was a male under the armor based on smell alone—had little chance of connecting, and while a kick had landed, the blow had failed to even damage his scales, much less the flesh beneath. They were engaged in a classic standoff, and he could only hope the man found it as frustrating as he did.

Cali's thoughts escaped her control, as they often did in battle, which allowed him to experience the fight from her perspective as well. He wished he could share senses better, but despite his attempts to broaden and deepen the connection between them, he hadn't been able to do so as yet. Somewhere deep in his memory, he knew more was possible but didn't know the correct route to get there. It was something to investigate once the battle was over.

He dodged another swipe of the man's sword, bit his forearm, and closed his teeth on the armor there. It gave a little and he yanked at the shell with a growl. He was surprised when the piece came free. There was a pause as they both realized what had happened before he breathed frost at his foe. Most of it was absorbed, but the man's hand and lower arm became trapped. With a hiss of pleasure at the discovery of his enemy's weakness, Fyre darted in to attack the armor on his legs.

Cali drove powerfully into her opponent and the magical momentum and the solidity of her arcane shield hurled the armored figure off its feet. She battered its helmet with her stick, then continued to do so until he stopped his attempts to recover. Quickly, she knelt beside her fallen opponent, pulled the helm off, and studied the young-looking man within. He was clearly unconscious. To be sure, she grasped his nose and yanked it, but he didn't react.

Okay, he's really out. Good.

She scrambled to her feet and took stock of the situation. Across the room, Fyre darted in to bite his opponent's legs while he avoided both sword and magical attacks with apparent ease. She stepped into the room where her stick had flown and called it to her hand, then crept along the wall toward her partner, out of the enemy's line of sight. The canny Draksa waited until she was close before he dodged with a small and deliberate stumble out of the small room he was in to entice the enemy to pursue him.

When the armored figure emerged, she repeated the process she'd used with the first one and hammered the helmeted head with her sticks until he fell. She yanked the helmet off to reveal another man and tested his awareness in the same way.

Together, she and Fyre removed the armor on the men's arms and legs and it took only a moment to bind the limbs with ice and render their foes formally incapacitated. She shook her head in annoyance.

"Buddy, I am so tired of this nonsense." The Draksa nodded but didn't offer any additional reply. With a sigh, she jogged in the direction from which they'd come to find the others as she announced, "Two down," over the comm.

Tanyith rushed to Zeb's side as he sheathed one Sai and replaced the weapon with a small force buckler to deflect any potential attacks. The dwarf still whirled his hand axes to absorb incoming magic, while he used his magic to fling objects from around the room at their foes. A cabinet ripped free from the wall and careened into the one on the right. The man staggered and Tanyith darted forward and thrust to full extension to pierce his armor with the Sai. It didn't go far enough to repeat the electrical trick, so he withdrew it and blocked the fire attack his enemy sent with the force buckler, which stretched and elongated to cover both him and his partner.

The dwarf stepped out from behind the shield for an instant and threw both of his axes. They streaked fast and hard on a line toward the left one's helmet, and his target's frantic efforts at dodge and deflection only managed to negate one of them. The other thunked into it and lodged there, and he fell. The remaining figure launched another blast of fire and turned to run, but neither of them was interested in a footrace. Tanyith's thrown Sai sank into the back of the runner's knee, and the examination bed his teammate hurled crushed the fleeing enemy between it and the wall.

Zeb wrenched his ax from the fallen man's helmet and held the weapon up to the light. The blade was clean. He made a satisfied sound. "Hard enough to ring his bell but not hard enough to kill him. Let's go find Cali."

She arrived moments before her two teammates and she nodded at them with a wide grin. Fyre sat on the floor and stared unblinkingly at Danna Cudon. She turned to the Atlantean leader and said, "A boon."

The woman slid from the table with a sigh. "Ask."

"A sit-down with you and your boss in neutral

territory."

She shook her head. "That is not mine to grant."

"I understand. Take it back and find out. If not, I'll ask something else. But this is a waste of time and effort for both of us, and there are much bigger matters to worry about."

Cudon gave a sharp laugh. "Perhaps all we really want is to see you dead."

The girl shrugged. "If so, I suppose it will be a very short conversation. But my guess is that there are other things you desire and maybe we can find a way to put this garbage behind us."

The woman stared at her for several seconds and her gaze bored into Cali's. Then, she turned and walked away. "I'll be in touch."

Zeb stepped beside Cali and observed, "Cold one, her."

"Only on the surface. I bet there's a lot going on under there."

He leaned closer and replied, "The same could be said for your friend over there." Her gaze followed his small gesture to where Tanyith crouched in the corner of the room. "He seemed very keen to take things a little further than necessarily required."

She nodded because she'd noticed similar behavior. "We all have so many challenges at the moment, I think. But we've won again, and that means a respite. Maybe longer than usual if it takes them extra time to fulfill my request. So hopefully, we'll have time to figure it out."

And if the stress of the Malniet situation is what's causing Tanyith's angst, I'll do what I have to do to get him out from under it.

CHAPTER TWELVE

C ali deliberately slowed her pace as she descended the long staircase into the basin of the Kemana, knowing that Fyre and Tanyith would both marvel at the surrounding sights. The Lady's palace glittered white at the far end of the enormous cavern, and the spoke-like streets stretched out from it like a child's drawing of the sun. The purple light from above filtered over everything, less intense than the last time she'd been there. *Twilight, maybe?* Regardless of the reason, it lent a sleepy look to the city, and the reduced traffic in the thoroughfares reinforced the image.

She pointed out the features she knew, the shops, the houses, the streets and sidewalks, and the location of Nylotte's shop. The others didn't speak as they followed her. After the final stair, she led them along the street that held Alessand's business, hoping it might be open so she could show them his amazing work. The locked door prohibited entrance, so she turned to head through an alley that connected to the lane the Drow's building was on.

"It's not quite what I described, except for the tunnel," Tanyith observed.

She shrugged. "I guess I've always been here in the daytime or something. I'm not sure Stonesreach follows the same clock that we do since there's no sun to divide the day." Fyre made a sound she took to be agreement, and she turned left as they reached the next road. A couple of dozen feet later, she grasped the handle of Nylotte's shop door, pulled it open, and preceded the others inside.

The main floor was empty, as she'd been told it would be. Stairs descending to the basement loomed before her, and she forced herself not to freeze in place.

I wouldn't want them to know how intimidated I am at the idea of Nylotte training me. No, never that. Even her internal laughter at herself was tinged with nervousness.

The staircase turned ninety degrees before it deposited her in a spacious room. A circle of metal set into the floor demarcated most of the area, with a small rectangle apparently reserved for storage at the side nearest the street.

The Drow sat in the lotus position slightly back from the center of the ring and looked at them with a smile. She gestured at the area in front of her. "Sit. Let's talk first."

She sat opposite the woman and tried not to stare as the others joined her, Fyre on her right and Tanyith on the left. The Dark Elf's white hair was bound into a high ponytail, and she wore all black—tall boots, leather pants, a tight tunic, and a thin leather jacket. Cali unconsciously tapped the silver rings on her thumbs and index fingers together at the sight of the five rings on Nylotte's hands.

The ring signifying leadership of House Leblanc was stored in New Atlantis, which left her one short of the other woman's count. She couldn't help but imagine it was deliberate, given the sense of control that radiated from her new mentor. The idea that the Drow might play mental games with those she chose to teach was not a huge leap beyond what she'd already experienced from her.

Cali grinned. "Thank you in advance for the lesson and for clearing the way for Fyre and Tay to join me."

The woman nodded. "Of course." She looked at the Draksa and then at Tanyith as if peering into their brains in search of secrets. Her attention returned to the girl after a few moments. "So, first, I have completed an initial reconnaissance of the area the dagger describes. It's an abandoned village deep in an Oriceran forest. I can't imagine how your parents found it. The engravings offered no greater clue as to where the supposed treasure lies within it."

She nodded and excitement surged inside. "Will you take me there?"

Nylotte chuckled. "Ah, your impulsiveness reminds me of my other student. Diana would have reacted the same way in your position. No, not yet. I mistrust the situation and have asked a friend to look into it. Remember that the blade was intended to be bait for you and although you may have avoided that trap, another might await."

Tanyith interrupted with a small frown. "Is it Chadrousse?"

"Of course."

Their exchange confused her until he turned to her and said, "Watch out for that one. He's very focused on racking up favors."

"Got it." She chuckled. "But if we need to know, we need to know."

Nylotte nodded. "That's how it starts. He is a master of what he does. Before you're aware of it, you're stuck performing an annoying task for him that merely leads to more trouble." She finished with a smile and a matching one appeared on Tanyith's face.

"Will you let me know as soon as you hear something?" she asked and let the worry go when she received a nod. "Okay. I can wait for a little longer, I guess, since I don't have a choice. Is there any news on the other blade fragments?"

The other woman shrugged. "Alessand believes your parents must have collected any engraved shards of metal they could find. He's sure there are fragments of another house sword included among them and quite likely a dagger identical to the one he's already reassembled. There's nothing incredibly useful at this time, however. Only acquiring more pieces will provide more insight."

"That's high on my list of priorities." Cali rummaged through the thoughts banging around her head and found nothing else in need of instant attention. "I think that's it."

The Drow rose gracefully to her feet, and she did the same, albeit with less style and agility. *But at least I'm better than Tanyith.* Her friend moved as if he was still sore from the battle the day before. Fyre, naturally, flowed like water as he stood.

"Anyone who doesn't wish to experience Caliste's efforts at controlling lightning should move outside the circle," her teacher warned. Her alleged allies were quick to find the opposite side of the metal ring.

"Traitors," she muttered and felt a wave of amusement from Fyre. She shifted her focus to the dark eyes of the woman in front of her. "You're not wrong, though. Emalia explained what I have to do—weave the lightning together into a tightly controlled line—but every time I try, it goes everywhere."

The Drow clasped her hands behind her back and nodded. "That is indeed one method but it's not the only possibility. Diana and I have had endless discussions about the fact that there are probably as many ways to use magic as there are people, and that a metaphor or understanding that works perfectly for one might be utterly insufficient for another." She looked a little startled and her teacher smiled. "It's entirely possible that you and your great aunt have different understandings of power, which makes her approach inappropriate for you."

The reflexive urge to defend Emalia summoned a snippy comment to her tongue despite the fact that her great aunt had said more or less the same thing, but she kept her mouth closed until it passed. "I can understand how that might be the case. How do you see it?"

The wide grin on the other woman's face suggested she had noted her restraint.

I wonder if Diana also always feels like she's being laughed at when she's around Nylotte. Maybe I'll ask next time I see her.

The Dark Elf's tone was crisp and teacherly, though. "For me, lightning isn't a thing to be controlled but rather coaxed and persuaded. I cannot make it do what I want but I can convince it to." She raised a hand and electricity surged from it in all directions before it coalesced into a ball that floated slightly above her palm.

Cali frowned. "How?"

Her teacher summoned another sphere of lightning and rotated them both above her palm. "For me, it is a matter of setting the power free with a clear vision of what I want it to become, then trusting it will do so."

"That's, like…the opposite of what Emalia said."

She nodded. "And she is not wrong. Neither am I. What works for her wouldn't work for me, and vice versa. If you want simple and predictable, you could always limit your-self to force magic." The condescension in her voice conveyed her opinion about that option.

"Right. Okay." Cali sighed. "Set it free and convince it to be what I want. Got it. How should I start?" She rolled her shoulders to ready herself for the attempt.

"By relaxing."

Her gaze snapped up to meet the other woman's. "What?"

"Relax, Caliste. This is not a battle. The magic is part of you, and the mindset of fighting yourself is not a useful one where power is concerned."

She muttered, "But I'm so good at it," as she forced herself to clench and release her muscles. When her body was calmer, she examined her thoughts and locked the troublesome ones away in their alcoves for later. When she felt she was ready, she nodded.

"Visualize what you want the lightning to become," Nylotte instructed. "Let's try for a sphere about the size of your hand. It's vital that you can see it before you release the magic."

Cali closed her eyes until the image appeared, then opened them and concentrated until her mental picture was superimposed over her palm like her teacher had done.

"Now, set your power free and concentrate on the ball."

She released it and lightning erupted to fill the entire area bounded by the metal. A shield shimmered around the Drow, and she called, "Now, envision it receding into the shape you've chosen."

Her mind had to make a sharp mental shift because she had waited to be called upon to dispel the magic and the unexpected instructions caught her by surprise. She tried pushing it into a sphere, then pulling, and when neither worked, remembered what Nylotte had said. Entirely focused, she imagined the power simply coming together as if by gravitational pull and condensing into the form she wanted. Around her, the tumult lessened, but she kept her concentration pure.

A sphere, about the size of my palm, made of electricity.

"An excellent first try." Her teacher clapped softly. Cali looked and grinned when she realized that, while it wasn't smooth or orderly like the Drow's had been, the power had more or less confined itself to the appropriate size and shape. She dispelled it and exhaled the breath she'd been holding.

"Okay, I think I understand."

"You've taken your first steps, anyway. It will require dozens more attempts before you're truly ready. So, you'd better get started." She groaned, and the other woman grinned. "You didn't think it would be easy, did you? Once you have the sphere mastered, the move to lightning whips will be a simple one. But you'll need to bifurcate your mind to keep them active while also using them to fight."

She nodded. "I've done that for other things. It should be the easier part."

"Good." She looked at Fyre and said, "Would you be so kind as to watch her and alert me if anything goes wrong? I'll leave the shield up to protect my store." The Draksa nodded and she turned to Tanyith. "You and I need to have a conversation. Come upstairs with me."

Cali watched them climb the stairs, wondered what the hell was going on, then packed that worry away with the others and focused on the task she'd been given.

Okay, lightning. Let's find a way to work together properly, shall we?

CHAPTER THIRTEEN

Nylotte followed Tanyith to the main floor, confident that the girl below wouldn't hurt herself. Her new student had learned fast and had significant potential to become quite proficient. She'd not worked with many Atlanteans in the past but had no reason to think Caliste's ancestry would be any hindrance to her accomplishment or to their ability to work together.

The ex-convict, however, was another issue. He seemed to be having challenges from what she'd been told and what she'd seen herself. Times had become too dangerous to let that situation continue. She had hoped it would be fixed without her involvement but waiting any longer for a resolution would be a bad idea.

At the top of the stairs, she brushed past him, pulled two stools from behind the counter, and gestured for him to take the one closer to the door. After her shop had been attacked, she'd sworn never to be caught even slightly off guard in it again, and that extended to not having her back to the entrance. She watched and waited for him to speak, a tactic that normally worked, but he seemed unable to do so. He shifted uncomfortably in the chair and didn't meet her gaze.

Finally, with a sigh, she asked, "What's the deal?"

He shrugged. "I don't know what you mean."

The Drow rolled her eyes. "Okay, let's dispense with the nonsense, shall we? I'm neither your therapist nor your doctor but clearly, something is the matter with you. I'd usually be content to let you work it out on your own, but there are bigger issues at play in which you hold a pivotal role. So. Speak and leave nothing out."

With a sigh, he raised his gaze from the floor. "Something's wrong with me." She resisted the urge to confirm it. "I endure low-level pain all the time and I have difficulty controlling my emotions."

She frowned. "Have you seen a doctor?"

The man shook his head. "I think it's simply stress. Ever since I met the damned Malniets and they put their hooks into me, that pressure is always present. I hate it." He all but snarled the last statement as if to emphasize his feelings.

"Uh-huh. Tell me more about the emotional part."

Tanyith shrugged. "I get angry faster, and I get angrier than I used to. Rage isn't something I really felt before, except for when I was sent to Trevilsom. Now, it's like an old friend."

"It seems logical that being falsely imprisoned could create that situation."

He gave a single dark laugh. "But it didn't manifest until we went to New Atlantis. If it had appeared before that, I'd believe it might be the cause. But no, I don't think so."

"So, if it's not physical and it's not emotional, there are only a few options left."

"Yeah. I'm losing my mind."

Nylotte shook her head. "That is doubtful, although I could question your choice of companions." She gave a small mocking smile and almost drew a matching one from him. "There's an unlikely possibility. Have you ever heard of a geas?"

He nodded. "In fantasy novels and ancient legends. Never for real."

"It's funny how what's real in one age passes for fiction in the next, and vice versa. But it's easy enough to find out. It might hurt a little, though."

Without waiting for permission, she spiraled her power toward him with the intention to read his. Barriers snapped up, doubtless by unconscious reflex, but it was a simple matter to envelop them while seeking a way inside. She'd practiced mental magic for decades, and this was not a particularly different process.

Absently, she noted the way his muscles locked as he fell off his seat, but it was a background happening and she didn't allow it to distract her. Finally, cleverly hidden within his magic, she found the parasitic spell. Tagging it so she could find it again easily, she released him.

He used the stool to pull himself from the floor and wiped the blood from where he'd split his lip. "A little, huh? That felt like being pounded with an electrified fireplace poker that had come out of the flames."

She laughed. "Very dramatic. You'll live. So the good news is that it's not physical or mental, although I can't claim you're wholly sound in either of those areas." The hopefulness that spread across his face was a pleasant sight.

"You're saying the bastards spelled me."

"Yes. Exactly." He rattled off a string of curses that demonstrated his problems with impulse control. While he did so, she saw the spell at work on him to push and hurt him in equal measure and drive his anger higher. She held a palm up and injected a tone of command into her voice. "Stop."

He obeyed reflexively, then realized what he'd been doing. He sat again, raised his hands, and let them drop. "Do you see what I mean?"

"I do. The bad news is that getting rid of it without giving the game away won't be easy. Dispelling it would be simple. However, eliminating most of the magic while ensuring your enemies don't know it's gone will require leaving some effects in place, although diminished."

"I understand." He nodded, his expression grim. "At this point, I'll take whatever I can get."

Nylotte grinned. "Excellent. You might want to lie on the floor for this, however." While Tanyith complied, she marshaled the magics she would require. It was a complicated task.

First, she would interrogate the existing spell to its most basic level to fully understand every part of it. Second, she'd need to craft her replica of the magic that would seem the same to those who had created it but have less of an effect on him, while incorporating enough of the original to fool its creator. Finally, she'd have to wipe away the first and put its replacement in more effectively than the man with the hat and the whip had in the movie

Diana's life-partner-troll Rath had insisted she watch with him.

Fortunately, she was the best user of magic she'd ever met. She cast a modified telekinesis spell to lock his limbs in place so he wouldn't hurt himself, then went to work on the important details.

It took her fifteen minutes to replace the enemy magic, then another five to rouse him to consciousness and get healing and energy potions into him. By the time he was ready to head down the stairs, the relief he felt was visible on his face.

"So, it's really gone?" he asked.

She nodded. "Mostly. Only a little was left to remind you to act hurt and upset and to fool those who put it on you. Definitely don't let them get close enough to examine you deeply, though."

Tanyith stretched and looked relieved. "I'll use Cali as my go-between. I could claim I'm hurting too much to come myself or something."

"That is a good plan. Speaking of which, go downstairs and make sure she hasn't killed herself or her mini-drag-on." He obeyed, and she straightened the stools and put the potion vials back where they belonged to be cleaned and refilled. When she'd finished, she turned to find the Draksa watching her. She frowned at him. "Is there something I can do for you?"

He nodded and spoke in an unexpectedly precise tone. "I kind of hope so."

With a sigh, she lowered herself to the floor so she could meet his gaze without straining her neck. He approached and sat again about two feet away from her. "Okay, what do you need?" she asked.

Uncertainty flickered across his expression and increased frustration colored his words. "To remember, I suppose. Or to know more about myself in whatever way I can. I have these feelings I can't quite take hold of but they tell me I should be able to forge a deeper connection with Cali and that we should be able to fight more effectively as a team. I don't know if I'm not able to do it because my memory is broken, or if my feelings are wrong, or if it's some other problem."

The Drow nodded. "I've refreshed my knowledge of Draksa since I first heard about you and researched more after I realized that you weren't an ordinary member of your species. Most of your kind can't talk in a way that non-Draksa can understand, for instance."

"It seems natural to me. It was only in New Atlantis that I discovered the others couldn't."

"It's certainly reasonable to assume that whatever makes you able to do the one might be involved in preventing you from doing the other. Or, if not so immediate a cause and effect, at least that they both stem from the same root. The problem is that it seems unlikely that we can dig into your memory to find out what that was."

His snout moved from side to side in an almost entrancing way as he shook his head. "It doesn't matter what it was. I'm happy with how things are now except that I want to be able to contribute more."

She frowned. "So. In order to help you with this, I have to know more. And since you can't tell me more, I'll need to use magic to investigate you. May I have your permission to do so?" He nodded, and she grinned. "And you're not worried about whether it will hurt or not? My last victim had issues in that area."

Fyre snorted. "Whatever it takes, that's what I'll do. Cali trusts you. Diana and Rath clearly trust you. I see no reason not to do the same."

The Dark Elf nodded. "I'll be as gentle as I can be. If you need me to stop, say so." He immediately curled on the floor and tucked his tail around his snout. It gave the impression that there was no chance he'd tell her to quit before she'd accomplished what he wanted. Her respect for the creature increased.

She stretched her magic out, enveloped him in it, and began to examine him without a particular goal in mind. Nylotte had learned over time that often, it was best to let the power flow with only the vaguest of intentions and trust that it would accomplish what was required—much the same approach she'd recommended to Cali for controlling lightning.

A distinct second energy radiated in him, like a strong memory that was too big to grasp. She would have thought it a geas, except it was ludicrous to think she'd run up against that twice in an hour and it also didn't quite taste the same. It was less a command than a subtle prompt. Not a spell, she realized, but something that was completely internalized. It was unlike anything she'd come across before.

But that doesn't mean I'm helpless in the face of it. She sought for the cracks in his mind to gain entry but found none. In the timeless place in which the magical experiment was conducted, she paused and considered her options. Finally, with a mental shrug, she tried to merge her magic with his at the outermost layer. It seemed to recognize her and permitted her access.

The problem was immediately obvious. The Draksa's mind was locked in conflict as the additional energy struggled with his native self. She didn't sense any antipathy or violence, only a mismatch of effort like rowers working against one another instead of in tandem. She couldn't identify the source of the extra magic and had no idea how to banish it.

What she could do, though, was to help him strengthen certain barriers and loosen others, essentially relegating his passenger to a different and less vital part of his mind. She did so, little by little, and coaxed his magic gently to assist. When she was finished, the powers were more in balance, although not perfectly so. She backed out slowly and made sure she left solidity in her wake.

When she finally returned fully to her body and opened her eyes, he was seated across from her, staring. "What did you do?" he asked. "I can feel a change already but I can't remember anything more."

She shrugged, unexpectedly tired from her efforts. "You have more than one magical essence inside you. They were combining in unbalanced ways, so I helped you to create a less conflicted arrangement. I don't promise it will last and I can't say we've found the full solution, but it's something."

Fyre smiled, and enthusiasm radiated from him. "That's what I felt. That makes sense now. And, yes, I think you've made things much better. Thank you. Thank you so much." He turned, raced to the stairs, and plunged down them at high speed.

Nylotte forced herself upright. To no one in particular, she muttered, "Your friendly neighborhood Drow amateur doctor and veterinarian, now open for business."

With a shake of her head, she followed the Draksa toward the basement. *Hopefully, Cali hasn't killed herself or Tanyith with the lightning. That would be a definite black mark on my teaching record.*

CHAPTER FOURTEEN

E mpress Shenni, in the deep blue formal robes more appropriate to the throne room she'd just left, smiled across the desk at her seneschal. The woman was many years older but still strong and attractive, clad in the palace's basic black with a wide stripe of blue down the left side of her long, martial-cut dress.

"So, what's this I hear about an altercation in the outer city?"

The other woman gave an answering grin. "It seems that a gang of mercenaries attacked the matriarch of House Leblanc and the patriarch of House Jehenel. It was most unexpected."

She nodded. "Indeed so. I presume the outcome was positive?"

Gwyn shrugged. "It depends on your perspective, Empress. For those rumored to have engaged them—House Cormier—it was likely not the result they hoped for. The hired soldiers were defeated very effectively. I'm told the matriarch's Draksa companion played a key role."

"That is an odd twist," Shenni replied and considered the creature that had bonded to the girl. "Has there ever been another occasion where the leader of one of the Nine had such a pet?"

The older woman chuckled. "More than a pet, certainly, Empress. But no, I found no record of such a pairing among the noble houses. Or in the palace." The way she raised her eyebrow at the end suggested she'd once again seen into her ruler's thoughts.

"Fine, yes, I might be a little jealous. It would be good to have such a companion as your responsibilities frequently take you from me. Plus, you're hardly obedient."

Gwyn laughed. "I obey to the degree my role requires, Empress. You could change my occupation, of course. I hear the consort position has yet to be filled."

The Empress snorted and chuckled. "Although I do treasure you, that would be a choice made for politics, not for pleasure." They both knew the other woman was only teasing but it was an amusing game. "Besides, you are too effective at what you do for me to even consider parting with your skills."

"Then you are doomed to be alone until you choose another, Empress." They both knew as well that she was only as lonely as she chose to be. She had no end of suitors to select from, all willing to serve for a night in hopes of gaining the prized plum of official recognition as her favorite.

She shook her head and frowned theatrically. "Woe, woe is me. So, what else do you hear?" The woman before her held the public role of seneschal, in charge of all things in the palace and responsible for making her ruler's will manifest, but also quietly served as her spymaster.

Gwyn leaned forward conspiratorially, despite the fact that no one else was present in the room. Shenni trusted her so completely that even her guards were not in position within those walls. "Action between the Malniets and Leblanc, of course. Devaux and Surette are quiet. Some whispers about what might happen if Malniet is weakened enough, either inside or outside the rules. The same for Leblanc."

"How many scions are left to House Malniet?"

"Three in the direct line. Some cousins who could be used as battle fodder."

Shenni leaned back in her chair and steepled her fingers as she considered the ramifications. "So, we can expect at least a few more rounds of conflict unless young Caliste is defeated."

Her seneschal nodded. "That's my understanding of the situation."

"And after that?"

"It is inconclusive."

The Empress grinned. "Indulge me."

The older woman straightened and paused before she spoke. "If either house should fall, the most likely outcome is that one of the other Nine will install a secondary family line in its place. Most have been building toward such a possibility since the failed attempt to destroy Leblanc years ago, so I would expect conflict among them for the opportunity."

She nodded. "Which works to my benefit. As long as they squabble with one another, they aren't acting against me. But having two houses with shared blood could prove to be a future problem. What are the options there?"

Gwyn frowned, the question clearly not one she'd prepared an answer for. "The only option to avoid that would be to support a third-party effort to join the nobility. However, such a thing has not happened since we set foot in New Atlantis."

Shenni waved a hand to dismiss that concern. "The Nine have been stagnant that whole time. Perhaps this is the right moment for new blood. Let's say that was something we wanted to promote. How might we do so?"

"The first step would certainly be to discover if there are any likely candidates. I shall start that process immediately."

The Empress leaned forward again. "But do so quietly—ever so quietly. We can't risk losing the support of the houses we trust, nor pushing away the ones whose loyalties are as yet unclear. I have no wish to see this fracas endanger my former house, nor see it threaten the monarchy." She chuckled. "I quite like it here, and there's so much left to do."

The woman raised an eyebrow. "You know you could sway loyalty in an instant by choosing a consort. Or, perhaps, even two."

With a wry grin, she echoed the other woman. "Such a thing has not happened since we set foot in New Atlantis."

Gwyn grinned and boldly imitated her ruler. "Perhaps this is the right moment, Empress."

With a laugh, she made a shooing motion with her hands. "Off with you. Summon the guards and give me a half-hour to finish here, then you may admit the patriarch of House Jehenel."

As she stood, the older woman said, "Speaking of excellent consort choices."

Shenni shook her head. "We already own his loyalty."

"You could always choose to bind him more closely."

"Away with you, matchmaker." Her seneschal departed and her laugh faded as she closed the door behind her.

To receive the representative of one of the nine noble houses of New Atlantis, the Empress chose to change from her less formal working robe into something more appropriate. The layers were rendered in her royal colors, a sheer black dress under a heavier and more luxurious scarlet gown. Her thick crimson locks were swept away from her face but hung freely down her back. She had cleared the desk of most nonessentials, and its empty wooden surface was bare except for a decanter, two glasses, and a small pile of paperwork on the right-hand side.

I don't want to appear too focused on my guest, after all, lest he get ideas.

It was a difficult line to walk, keeping her many admirers—or, to be more specific, those wishing to influence her in matters of power and treasure—on a leash short enough to maintain their interest but long enough to not provide them sure footing. Fortunately, she'd had years of practice and had developed keen instincts. Also, she was almost certain Gwyn used one of her guards as an information source to keep her updated on potential problems.

When he entered, Wymarc Jehenel appeared none the worse for wear. His sharp features and gorgeous eyes drew attention to his face immediately. His clothing choices had a certain tightness in common as if he wanted to display what was beneath in a not particularly subtle way. Black trousers that looked as if they'd be very soft to the touch clung to the outlines of his leg muscles until they vanished into supple leather boots, and a pale yellow tunic wrapped him like a second skin. His arms were bare and stood out so much that he might have lifted weights in the hallway before he entered. All in all, he made a fetching display but a rather obvious one.

She extended her hand, and he knelt beside her to kiss it, then took the chair on the opposite side of the desk at her gesture. His gaze was locked on her face with an intensity she might have found threatening in one she didn't share secrets with.

He smiled widely. "Empress Shenni, thank you for agreeing to meet with me yet again. I am surely the most fortunate of your subjects."

Her first instinct was to roll her eyes at him but she lowered her gaze and covered her mockery by reaching for the decanter. "But of course, Patriarch Wymarc." She poured for them both, a notable honor for her guest, and nudged the glass of dark rum toward him. He waited while she sipped hers and sighed in pleasure at the sharp taste and the warm burn that followed.

Wymarc mirrored her actions, then set the tumbler on the table. "So, what shall we discuss?"

Shenni smiled at the weak gambit. "How about you tell me about your adventure the other evening?"

The young patriarch nodded and returned his head to the perfect angle for admiring. *I bet he practices in the mirror.* She couldn't be too scathing about it as she did the same thing. One's body was as much a communication device as one's voice in the circles she frequented.

"I was having a lovely night out with Matriarch Leblanc when we were set upon by ruffians. Fortunately, we were able to defeat them without lasting injury."

She chuckled. "You are a master of understatement. From what I hear, it was a more significant fight than you suggest and the girl's Draksa proved pivotal."

He shrugged, and his soft smile didn't change. "All battles are significant, Empress. But I don't believe we were in any true danger. It felt more like a focused warning than an earnest attempt on our lives."

"House Devaux, was it?"

"No, according to the mercenary leader, it was Cormier."

"Odd." Shenni tilted her head. "Cormier seems to gain little from doing such a thing, at least where the Leblanc family is concerned. Does House Jehenel have issues with Cormier?"

"None that I know of, Empress." The way he said it confirmed her suspicion.

"Then you were behind it and blamed it on them." It was a statement, not a question, and he nodded in reply. "To what end?"

"Multiple positive outcomes, Empress. First, Cormier is implicated. For a house that supports you to appear to take action against Caliste will confuse her. It may also offer you an opportunity to further secure their loyalty in the face of this false accusation by the mercenary captain." His tone became more noble and prissy as he spoke, and she laughed as he finished.

"Indeed so. They have already requested an audience. What else?"

He took a sip of his drink before he replied. "Second, I am cemented in her eyes as an ally. We've fought together and defended one another. This can only increase her trust and thus my influence upon her as matters progress."

"That seems logical." She was careful to neither approve nor disapprove.

"Finally, and perhaps most importantly, it will build her perceived sense of danger while in the city. That, in turn, may cause her to act more quickly or with less considera-tion of all the consequences of her actions, or both. Regardless, the level of uncertainty and chaos inherent in her interactions here is increased."

The Empress smiled. "I can only agree with you on all these points. It was well done, Wymarc." He nodded and looked satisfied, and she added. "So, have you managed to find your way into the girl's bed yet?"

His fixed stare was the only sign that her question had surprised him. "I was unaware that was part of what you wished from me, Empress."

She laughed. "Oh, it's not. I merely assumed you would avail yourself of the opportunity provided to become one of the girl's trusted inner circle."

He shook his head. "Honestly, she doesn't interest me in

that way. While she's attractive enough, I prefer my partners a little more sophisticated."

"That's not what I hear, Wymarc. Quite the opposite, in fact. I have been told you are...um, shall we say less than discerning?"

The young man grinned and laughed to display perfect teeth. "Ah, Empress Shenni, you speak of another man. One who was younger and stupider. But now that I have had the opportunity to spend time with you and we have found a common cause, I find myself changed. My interests are much more focused."

Well said, courtier. She smiled. "Well. That is good to hear, Patriarch Jehenel." She raised her glass. "To remaining focused on that which is important."

In your case, the girl and making sure that whatever she's up to doesn't blow back on your ruler.

CHAPTER FIFTEEN

Ozahl, formerly Aiden Walsh, wore the disguise of a businessman today. His illusory body was heavier than his own and strained at the seams of the boring brown suit he had chosen. His hair was brown, as was the ludicrous mustache he'd added. When he took the seat across from Danna Cudon, she stifled a laugh.

"I will have numerous people questioning why I would date this person."

He grinned. "Tell them I possess a sparkling personality." The woman looked as beautiful as always in her sharp-lined charcoal pinstripe suit and red power tie over a white shirt. She'd added light makeup, and her hair was slicked back in kind of an Annie Lennox from the eighties style. He appreciated the effort but it was never necessary. His love for her and his attraction to her never wavered even a centimeter.

"It would have to be. Although I like the facial hair a little."

The mage held his reply when the waiter arrived. He

decided the person he impersonated would be a gin and tonic guy and a chicken eater, so he ordered those. Danna selected a martini with extra olives and a steak, medium-rare. The server departed with a prim, "Very good."

"Did you have a positive day today?" Ozahl asked.

She shrugged. "Mondays are always a little slow. The demand over the weekend means a smaller supply, so we only take care of the most important customers today. Of course, they all want one-on-one time, so I must be attentive and oh-so-interested." She made a face like the one he assumed she wore to give that impression, and he laughed because it so wasn't her.

"It's all in the game, my love, and you play it well."

Danna nodded. "We play it well." She leaned forward and spoke softly so her voice wouldn't carry. "Speaking of which, have you come up with a final plan?" They'd discussed options during every moment together over the weekend, but the ultimate decisions were still his since they involved the Zatoras more than they did the Atlanteans. Such was their agreement at the outset, and it had served them well thus far.

The arrival of their drinks and a basket of hot bread interrupted the conversation until they had been sampled and appreciated. He decided the body he wore was the kind to have a second roll and he spread butter on it while he answered the question. "I have. I think it's solid—definitely ready for you to rip it apart." He said the last with a smile. It was another part of their process to try to find flaws in the other's plans.

"Hit me."

"So, we want two things out of this. Well, three really,

but the third is a product of the others. First, we need to fire one of the man's lieutenants." The man was Rion Grisham, leader of the Zatora syndicate, but it would be bad form to say that out loud. Equally bad would have been saying "kill" instead of "fire," which was far more accurate.

Danna sipped her drink and he lost himself for a moment in her red lips. "Agreed," she said. "And the second thing?"

He grinned. "To pin it on our favorite person." Their efforts needed to stay hidden so if they could contrive to put Caliste Leblanc into the situation, it would provide cover as everyone involved was already inclined to distrust her. "Those things will conceal our involvement and sow chaos among our competitors. All our competitors." *Above the surface and below.*

She detached an olive from its toothpick with perfect teeth and chewed it in silence for a moment. He busied himself with the remains of his second roll. Finally, she said, "Okay. To the first point. Have you chosen?"

Ozahl nodded. "The accountant, if possible. Either will work, but the other is far more easily replaced." Colin Todd was the smarter of Grisham's lieutenants. He was also the one who he often caught sending strange looks his way as if he sensed that the Zatora's pet mage wasn't nearly as obedient or dedicated as he seemed. "Plus, he's kind of a smug jerk."

Her smile appeared in an instant. "And that's a perfect rationale, right?"

"I can think of worse ones."

Danna grew serious. "And do you think our favorite person will handle the firing?"

He shook his head. "If we get lucky, we get lucky, but it's far too risky to leave that to chance. I'll be there to take care of it if needed." He'd considered impersonating her and doing the whole thing himself, but it would be much better if clear and unmistakable evidence of her involvement existed. Having her there in person would strengthen the case substantially.

"Okay. I guess the only problem I see with that is how you get her to attend the meeting. I presume you have something in mind?"

"The best bait. She's searched for pieces of the...uh, family heirloom that was broken, right?" She nodded. They'd discussed how Caliste had avoided the trap set around the delivery of the dagger piece and how her actions showed it was useful bait. "Well, the boss man has one. He's a collector and all. It should be simple to create a scenario to draw her in."

The mage paused as the waiter placed a chicken breast covered in mushrooms and dark sauce accompanied by a mound of mashed potatoes in front of him. Danna's steak followed, and he gave them each a sharp knife before he departed. He tasted his and grinned. "This is a great choice of restaurant. It's delicious."

She tried her steak and nodded. "This is good too. Definitely a win. I'll have to come here again with someone else sometime if this date doesn't work out."

He laughed. "I don't think we'll be long term, I'm afraid. My suit is too tight."

"So, back to the important details. How do you think you'll get our favorite person to accept the gig in the time-frame we need? It's not exactly local and she probably has misgivings about the company."

To say that Caliste had issues with the Zatoras was likely the understatement of the year and he suppressed a laugh. "Scarcity rules. We'll let her know that the item will be off the market in short order so she has to act now."

She sighed and tapped the edge of her martini glass with a nail. "Okay, I don't see problems with those. However, on my side of things, my boss needs to believe that I took care of this, right? So, how do you plan to make that happen? Surely you haven't forgotten about my career?" Danna's grin was teasing.

"Of course not. I thought perhaps simultaneous action to create even more chaos. We bring your company in to add pressure to the situation at the same time we have her there. It would probably work better if they arrive a little later. If we're lucky, the fallout might solve all kinds of problems for us."

The woman chewed thoughtfully, then shook her head. "It won't work. It would give up the next phase of the rollout if my company was seen to be involved. We need a different idea."

Now it was his turn to think, and he ate most of his chicken while he worked on the problem. They'd collaborated enough that she knew how he dealt with things and didn't interrupt his mind while it reviewed and discarded possible solutions. Finally, he had it, and set his utensils down with a grin.

"Okay, how about this, then? Tell your boss you have a source on the inside who revealed that they will leave their current location for a new one. Then, suggest that our favorite person might care about that and with the right words, she might even take care of the setup for the second part for you."

Her eyes lit with approval. "And we can use the sit-down to either share that outright or let it slip. That's a great idea. It seems like everyone wins."

Ozahl chuckled. "Well, almost everyone. But we'll need a backup plan in case you can't get the word to her. Maybe the council. The man has an issue with them anyway so we might be able to plant it there somehow."

She shrugged. "One doesn't preclude the other. We can do both."

They ordered coffee and desserts and traded mouthfuls of their selections exactly like folks on a date would. When they were finished, they left together and walked onto the main street in New Orleans' Garden District.

"Do you feel like a wander?" he asked. She nodded and fell into step beside him as he walked slowly farther into the commercial area. After a couple of minutes of silence, he leaned toward her. "Are you okay?"

Danna nodded. "Fine. I still wish we could resolve this quickly and go home but I understand that's not in the cards. So, this is good. And if it heads off an effort to remove my boss, even better."

He'd told her about Grisham's intention to eliminate Usha, and while he personally didn't care too much, she had strong positive feelings for the woman. His helpers had already fulfilled their assignments, one of which involved putting together a plan to assassinate her based on watching her movements for several days. Ozahl held it back from Grisham until he had to reveal it. He'd handled the other task to identify a target on the magical council himself but had been reinforced by their efforts.

"Don't worry. I won't let that happen, at least not anytime soon. And it's not something he'd try without me, I'm sure." Dalton and Lila were keeping an eye on that situation as well and would alert him if any action was planned. Even though he thrived on the plots and the chaos, he also longed to move into the next phase of their plan where they took control of a noble house and made it their own. "Soon, love. Soon, we will have what we've worked toward for so long."

She nodded. "I believe you. Now, how about we split up so no one thinks we're going home together and meet in your apartment in an hour?"

The mage grinned. "It's the best offer I've had all day. Should I keep the mustache?"

Laughter was the only reply.

CHAPTER SIXTEEN

His irritation exceeded normal bounds when he was summoned by Colin Todd to attend a meeting with Grisham at the mansion. He decided the big man was sending him a message by having his lieutenant communicate for him.

One more reason to kill him. One more reason to kill them both. With the vicious thought suppressed, he slipped his normal disguise on and portaled obediently to his boss's home.

The building's security remained impressive and he was noticed immediately when he stepped out of the bedroom he used as his access point. The room was inaccessible by anyone other than him as he locked it whenever he entered or left and no key existed. Only his telekinesis permitted access. Of course, they could remove the door, but that would trip the wards he'd placed on it and alert him to their efforts.

The guards stepped forward but returned to their positions once they recognized him. No one in the organization knew how easily he could impersonate any of them and it amused him to imagine doing so. Strolling through the hallways as Grisham would have its benefits.

And I might wind up having to do that before we're done with these people, who knows? He shook his head and headed down the stairs to the first floor.

The Zatora leader was in the dining room with Jack Strang and Todd. Dark curtains covered the windows to block out the late afternoon sun, and the trio stared at a laptop screen. On it was displayed an aerial view of a street he didn't recognize.

"Is this a Google maps party?" he asked. The three men scowled at him, which immediately pushed up his annoyance level with all of them.

Strang responded, his tone belligerent. "It's a drone. Over the target's house."

He stepped forward for a closer look. The buildings on the monitor were all similar enough to be essentially the same and minimal activity showed nearby. "Which one did you choose?"

Grisham laughed. "Always start at the top, that's my motto."

Ozahl nodded. He would have made the same selection, which was simultaneously reassuring and annoying. "Do you see anything of concern?"

Todd shook his head. "It's a boring location, honestly. There aren't many cars or many pedestrians, and not even people walking dogs. If there's a less interesting place in all New Orleans, I can't imagine what it looks like."

The other humans chuckled, and the mage shrugged.

When you can portal, where you live isn't all that relevant. "So, what's the plan?"

Strang grinned. "You're the plan, buddy."

Grisham added, "Yep. Get whoever you need and go in and take him out. Ten o'clock tonight. We'll be watching. Hell, maybe we'll make popcorn and put it on a big screen." The three men laughed together and he again resisted the urge to drop a fireball on them. His plans were too important to let himself indulge random desires, however.

He grinned. "I'd be happy to."

His first stop was his home. He changed into pants with numerous pockets and filled them with useful items—extra potions, large zip-ties, cloth to use as a gag or blindfold, and a burner phone in case. He'd have to wear his Zatora disguise during the op, unfortunately, but it couldn't be avoided.

Unless I did it alone but I don't want them to know I'm that powerful. And besides, giving the enemy someone else to aim at is always an advantage.

His associates weren't in the first two venues he tried, but enough Zatoras were that he acquired directions to find them. He found them at a public firing range, working their way through a series of weapons he didn't recognize. On surfaces around them lay extra-large pistols, rifles, and unexpectedly tiny guns that looked like the kind of thing a rich woman might hide in a clutch purse. He waited until they had fired their weapons dry, then tapped them both on the shoulder. They turned, looking amusing in their heavy sound-protection earphones, and he pointed at the door and touched his watch. Each nodded, and he went outside to wait.

They joined him in less than five minutes, as responsive to his orders as they always were. Lila wore jeans and a leather jacket, and the black material contrasted perfectly with the light blonde hair that fell loosely around her face. "What's up, boss?" she asked.

"We have a job. The council member we've been preparing for."

Dalton, looking as always like a stockbroker heading to happy hour, grinned. "Excellent. Do we have time to stop for gear?"

"Yep," Ozahl replied. "We strike at ten sharp so we have an hour to get into place."

Lila's smile matched her partner's. "You always bring us the best jobs. The car's this way."

Eight minutes shy of an hour later, they were in position at the end of the block that the council leader, one Vizidus, lived on. The neighborhood was as uniform and dull as it had appeared from the drone. The camera platform was barely visible in the high distance, still roughly positioned over the house.

Way to give him advance warning, assuming he notices. Idiots. The mage shook his head and opened the car door.

The others followed him down the street. Each had gone into their apartment dressed casually and returned outfitted for a fight. They had made identical choices—

black trousers with extra pockets, heavy boots, dark t-shirts, and black leather jackets. He'd noticed guns in shoulder holsters and presumed they carried any number of other weapons as well.

Hopefully, they wouldn't be needed. In truth, there was no reason to think the man would be able to offer any substantial defense against his magic. Even if he somehow proved to be equal in magical ability, Ozahl knew so many more tricks than anyone he'd ever met that it should make defeating the other wizard easy.

They turned together to march up the short walk to the house and he raised a hand. A blast of force streaked out to strike the front door, but it did not fly off its hinges or splinter into pieces as he'd expected. Instead, wards activated to dissipate his attack. He shrugged. "You're up." He focused his attention on identifying and deactivating the house's arcane protections as his people stepped forward.

By the time they reached the door, he'd done away with the magical defenses. The heavy shotgun that Lila drew from under her jacket removed the handle and the lock above it and Dalton kicked the flimsy wooden barrier open. In the next moment, he catapulted back. Ozahl slipped calmly out of his path, used telekinesis to cushion his landing, and ran toward the entrance. He managed to raise a shield in front of Lila seconds before the lightning struck and protected her from the cascade of burning energy.

Vizidus stood in the doorway that connected the living room to the dining room, his hair askew and wearing what looked like striped pajamas of a style that hadn't been popular in decades, if not centuries. He held a wand in a steady hand, although the rest of his body trembled in either fear or outrage. The younger man decided it was more likely the second. He launched an attack of his own, and the wizard created a large circle of force that intercepted his shadow bolts and rebounded them toward Lila. His shield again proved adequate to protect her from the assault.

"Give it up, old man," he shouted, and whispered to the woman beside him, "Go left and try to get behind him." His subordinate darted out of the room as Dalton reentered it and fired his pistol at the aged wizard. The defender's barrier didn't waver and the force disc prevented each of the rounds from reaching him. Motion from his left drew Ozahl's attention and a woman he didn't recognize raised a wand. He called a pair of shields and positioned them to face each of the opposing magicals to absorb their coordinated attack without difficulty.

Vizidus snapped, "Get out of my house, bastard, or we'll take the gloves off."

He laughed. "Please. I could kill you both and not break a sweat. But I'm only here for you, councilman, to deliver a farewell from Rion Grisham. Your friend here can leave safely if you give up."

She responded by blasting the floor under his feet and the mage dropped into a basement and landed with a hard crash. Such a move hadn't even entered his mind, and a part of him applauded her effort. *Too bad it won't change the outcome.* Already, he heard shouts and gunfire from above, and as long as Lila and Dalton kept them occupied, he should be able to strike from an unexpected direction and eliminate them.

The stairs were easy to find, and he climbed them quickly and reached a kitchen filled with appliances as old as the wizard's pajamas. He crouched and made his way quietly toward the dining room, where the witch stood back to back with the wizard. Their eyes met, and as she snarled and extended her wand, he abandoned the initial plan to let her live to plant the clue about Grisham leaving the mansion. He reached out with his power and yanked the ceiling down on them both.

A cascade of wood, drywall, and furniture buried them. Each managed a shout of surprise, but anything more was lost in the sound of the avalanche. When it finished, he expected to see body parts in the rubble, but none were visible. He frowned and gestured, and the material began to unstack itself. The notion that they might not be under there pressed at the edge of his mind, but he wasn't prepared to acknowledge it yet. If they weren't and he had to listen to Grisham whine about it, he would find it very difficult to not kill the man.

Zeb had barely begun to clean when he sensed the emergency portal location downstairs activate. As events in New Orleans had accelerated, he'd decided to make one more area of the Drunken Dragons Tavern accessible to others, but only on a limited basis. The council members could transport themselves to the corner of the basement but would be hemmed in by his magics until he arrived to release them. Its use was not a good sign.

He raced down the stairs as fast as his legs would carry

him. Vizidus and his wife waited within the transparent magical walls, both covered in dust and the prone wizard also smeared with blood. He dispelled the wards and ran to them, retrieved his healing potions, and handed them to Tracia. She dribbled it into her husband's mouth, then helped him to sit and drink more. By the time the vial had been emptied, he had a glass of water for each of them. He escorted them up the stairs and seated the couple at a table, then sat across from them. Even though the potion had done its work, they both looked weary.

"What happened?" he asked,

Vizidus coughed. "No good deed goes unpunished, my friend. Apparently, the Zatoras have an issue with the council."

The dwarf frowned. "Why do you say that?"

"The magical that dropped our house on us said so," Tracia replied acidly. "'A farewell from Rion Grisham.' I suppose it's too much to hope he meant the bastard is leaving town."

The wizard laughed. "That is doubtful. It's more likely that he's concluded we're an impediment to his plans and decided it was time to do something about it."

Zeb shook his head. "This doesn't make sense. The council hasn't done anything to him directly. I wonder why?"

The old man snorted. "He's gone crazy with power, is what it is. What more is there to say? He's afraid of anyone who won't do what he says so he lashes out. Well, he made a mistake when he didn't finish the job. We need to bring the others together. It's time to take action."

The dwarf sat with the couple until they were ready to

walk to a hotel. All of them agreed that it would be a bad idea to return to the house with anything other than a full force. As he left them at the entrance to the Sheraton and turned to stroll back through the Quarter, he shook his head.

There's something more going on here and I don't think it bodes well for any of us.

CHAPTER SEVENTEEN

The text message summoning him to The Otter had been unexpected but welcome. Most of Tanyith's efforts to find Aiden Walsh had so far been unsuccessful, but he'd also dropped a few lines into the water to see what would bite, as his father used to say. That Karam had reached out to ask for a meet to share information gave him hope that at least one of his rods had snagged a fish.

He had to pause at the landing to let a drunken couple pass and grinned inwardly. They hung on to one another and it seemed to indicate the seemingly uncomplicated pleasure they took in the other's company. *No doubt there's a world of challenges an inch below the surface like there are for all of us. Still, it's nice to see romance flourish, if only for a moment.* He made it the rest of the way up the narrow staircase without challenge.

The bar had a solid crowd for ten on a Wednesday night with even more people around than he remembered from the days when it had been one of the Atlantean gang's secondary hangouts. For a minute, he wondered what Zeb would make of it as it seemed a polar opposite to the tavern. Individuals and small groups shared drinks in huddles as opposed to the air of celebration that usually filled the Drunken Dragons' common area. Unless Cali was fighting with someone, of course.

He grinned at the thought of his partner in...well, certainly not crime, regardless of Barton's opinion. *Justice, maybe.* He chuckled inwardly. *It would take a better poet than me to find the answers to that.* An arm waved from the far corner of the room opposite the entrance, the last table along the big windows that looked out over the street below. He snatched the drink Otto set on the bar for him as he neared and headed over and took the chair across from his oldest friend and mentor.

Karam nodded. "Thanks for coming."

"Well, when you use the words 'meet' and 'information' in the same text message, how could I resist?"

The older man lifted his glass to his lips. Like last time, he was richly dressed in a shirt that shimmered in blue and black trousers and shoes that sucked in the light. His dreads were pulled away from his face. "I thought that would catch your attention. But before I tell you what I discovered, I might suggest that you should let this whole thing go right now. You won't get any more money out of it, true?"

Tanyith chuckled. "No, that well is dry and besides, I already have what I was promised. The lack is on my end since I haven't delivered the answers yet."

The other man shook his head. "You know, answers sometimes aren't all they're cracked up to be. Especially where it concerns the past. It might be better to let things that are buried stay buried."

"Sorry. I can't do it. I had this role model once who wouldn't let anything go once he'd committed to it. He kind of resembled you around the face and eyes, now that I think of it, and he taught me well."

Karam laughed and his deep voice attracted the attention of those nearby, who stared for a moment before they returned to their conversations. The older man nodded. "Yeah, I guess that sounds like me, doesn't it? Okay, here's what I know—and mind you, this is sixth- or seventh-hand information. There is all kinds of 'I know a guy' happening in this chain of knowledge."

He shrugged. "I won't hold you accountable for its accuracy. And really, anything is better than the nothing I have right now."

"Okay. The word is there's a warehouse."

"What the hell is it with warehouses?" he interrupted, then laughed. "Sorry, that's a long story. Let me get refills." He crossed to the bar and took the new glasses in exchange for the empties and sat again. "So, you were saying?"

"Right. There is apparently a warehouse, up to the north. Someone from the old days said they'd overheard a conversation that sounded like how Aiden talked, even though the person didn't look anything like him. They managed to trail him, probably looking to skim off whatever he was up to. Walsh was always good at finding money."

Tanyith chuckled softly. "Yeah, and constantly so secretive about how he did it. The bastard."

Karam nodded. "Anyway, they followed him to this

warehouse and discovered more than they expected. Now I'm not really up on the players these days, but the source said they were Zatoras."

He frowned. "First, don't give me that. You know everything that's happening around here—always have and always will. But second, let me make sure I have this straight. You're suggesting our old friend is tied up with a gang of anti-magical humans?"

His mentor spread his hands wide and leaned back in his chair. "Exactly that. And it was my reaction too. Like, seriously, what the hell?" He shook his head. "But it's a crazy world and getting crazier. It's not out of the question. And like you said, there's always something hidden with our friend Aiden Walsh." He fumbled in his shirt pocket for a pen, found a napkin, and wrote an address on it. "Here's the location. But I'm telling you, if this was my search, I'd give it up and find myself a new girlfriend."

Tanyith picked it up, looked at it once, and folded it and slid it into the back pocket of his jeans. "She's not my girlfriend anymore and won't be again. But I still need to do what I said I'd do."

Karam stared at him hard for a minute before he broke into a grin. "No, you simply need to know because you're damned curious about everything and can't let a secret exist without trying to find out what it is. Same as always."

He pointed at the older man. "That's unfair and entirely probable." They shared a laugh and he swallowed the rest of his drink. "Okay. I guess I have some investigating to do. Thanks, man."

His oldest friend nodded and they exchanged fist

bumps. Tanyith threw two twenties on the bar and headed to the door.

Maybe once I put this to rest, I can get myself some investigative work that actually pays me money, rather than costing me.

For the first time in weeks, he had the feeling he was finally on the right track.

He'd made the trek to the particular part of town in an Uber and had suffered through a long diatribe from the driver about how the New Orleans Saints needed to move on from their quarterback. His knowledge of football was far from encyclopedic, but he was fairly sure that wasn't the issue with the team, given the other chatter he'd heard.

Once he'd escaped from that particular discomfort, he'd proceeded the last several blocks on foot and waited to be sure the car would have ample time to clear the area in case anyone tried to back-trace his movements.

Not that I'll get caught but it doesn't hurt to cover all the bases.

Tanyith selected his favorite option and took to the roofs when he was close and made his way undetected to the building parallel to the warehouse. He crouched and scuttled carefully across it until he approached the side that looked onto his target. The roof had no wall, so he zipped his leather coat and lay on the gravel surface to wiggle forward until he could see the structure he was interested in.

It rose three stories high, the same as the one he was on.

Signs of activity abounded, with several trucks pulled up to the loading docks and the sounds of workers unloading them. It seemed rather less than secretive and completely the opposite of what he'd expected. As far as he knew, the Zatora syndicate had no public-face cover business that would justify what happened below.

Well, it's not like I know everything about them. And it's so deserted around here that maybe they simply don't care.

He watched for fifteen minutes to get a sense of the ebb and flow of the people inside. Like the roof he was on, skylights dotted the top of the other building, which he assumed would offer the safest route to get a decent look inside. He extended his magical senses to search for traps or wards but found none. With a frown, he tried again but the result was the same.

Okay, I'd better be on the lookout for physical defenses. He spent another fifteen minutes scanning his target carefully, half-afraid that he'd already been detected by an electronic device he couldn't see. But that also came up empty—no cameras, no obvious tripwires, and no blocks that looked like they could be laser beam sensors.

Maybe they rely on secrecy? He shrugged, having considered all the possibilities he could think of. *There isn't much more I can do.*

Tanyith waited until the workers below had all entered the building once more and launched himself across the street. He used a combination of telekinesis and force magic to land lightly and immediately dropped to his stomach again, ready to summon a portal and vanish at any sign that he'd been noticed. After several minutes, he low-crawled to a skylight and peered into the warehouse.

It appeared to be a typical storage area, much like what he'd seen at the local big-box hardware store, with rows of shelves separated by barely enough space to drive a forklift between them. It was only a quarter filled, and he couldn't discern any labels on the crates. They looked as if they'd been there for a long time, though. He crabbed a little to get a better angle on the loading dock, and things finally started to make a little sense.

A different storage arrangement was present there where crates were stacked atop one another in a grid pattern, sized for hand jacks rather than motorized forklifts. The workers removed boxes from pallets and placed them on separate stacks. Many had stenciled letters in army green, while others were unmarked. Some of the former were labeled *MRE* and others marked as *ammunition.*

So they are either stealing from the nearby bases or working a black-market scam. That's consistent. Heavy plastic cases stood in the far section and as he turned his attention to them, three men walked into view, headed to that area. The first looked like a lawyer or accountant with mousey brown hair and a stylish tan suit. He was in conversation with a second and much larger man dressed in a less expensive suit that didn't fit nearly as well as his friend's. His status as a gym rat was apparent even from a distance. The two stopped walking but continued to talk and gestured toward the boxes in front of them.

The third man seized his attention the instant he strode into view. He could get lost in a crowd even faster than the first. Everything about him was ordinary, from the sandy hair to the ill-fitting shirt, pants, and sweater vest he wore.

But none of those had arrested his senses. It was, instead, the way he moved and the slight quirk at the end of the smile plastered on his face. Those were as familiar to Tanyith as Kendra's grin or Zeb's scowl. He'd spent hours at a time with the guy back in the day, and those characteristics were clear identification, regardless of the clothes and skin he wore.

"Aiden Walsh, you damn bastard," he muttered. "What the hell are you doing hanging out with these scumbags?"

He couldn't get inside without notice, not with a magical of Walsh's skill present. *Hell, I'm lucky I haven't been noticed yet.* His mind spun plans to follow the man, but he was in no way ready for that. It would require preparation but now, he finally knew something. Not only that, but he also had an idea of how to put a crimp in the gang's plans, or at least a small one.

Quickly and quietly, he moved away from the skylight, launched himself to the other rooftop, and called Kendra. "There'll be a report of a fire in a few minutes." He gave her the address. "You'll want to roll on it. The building has some interesting contents." She replied in the affirmative and hung up. Her penchant for quick action was one of the many things he liked about her.

Tanyith retrieved the burner phone he always carried and turned it on. He dialed nine-one-one and made an effort to disguise his voice with something close to low and growly. "Yah, there's a fire here." He shared the location and clicked off, yanked the sim chip out of the device, and incinerated it with a brief burst of fire magic. Then, with a smile for the chaos he hoped he'd caused, he delivered a fireball into the corner of the building farthest from the workers. It had little chance of spreading but a great chance that the fire department and police would arrive in time to find the illicit goods.

When the shouting began, he portaled away, satisfied with his night's work.

CHAPTER EIGHTEEN

S coppic had been able to narrow down the location of
the museum Emalia had identified. It was in the Latin
quarter of Paris, home to the Sorbonne and other national
treasures. The gallery that allegedly contained the shard
was part of the National Museum of Natural History.
Dasante had scoured the web and downloaded floor plans
and maps for her and had even offered to come.

She felt no small regret about the way the events of her
life had pulled her apart from her older friends and
pursuits and seriously missed busking in Jackson Square
with her neighbor. But she'd forced herself to pack those
thoughts away for later, with the distinct hope that there
would be a later in which to unpack them.

Although the magical council could have gotten her to
Paris, Nylotte deemed the situation worthy of reaching out
to her other students. Cali, Tanyith, Fyre, and Zeb now
waited in the tavern for their arrival, far earlier in the
morning than any of them likely would have wished. Tay

looked pleased about something and seemed to carry less stress than he had in the recent past. She wanted to push him to talk but experience had taught her that he'd share in his own time or not at all, and trying to change that would merely make him grumpy. Instead, she contented herself with stew, cider, and waiting.

Finally, a noise emanated from below and they all turned expectantly toward the stairs, except for Fyre who barreled out from behind the bar to sit at the top. Rath appeared first, his purple hair a blur as his three-foot form hurtled through the air to wrap the Draksa in a hug. Fyre fell back and while the two wrestled, the troll's laughter filled the room and summoned smiles to every face.

Next up the stairs was Diana Sheen, the leader of the agents. She was dressed in casual black jeans, boots, and a t-shirt under a thin leather jacket, and carried a black backpack. Now clipped almost to the scalp at the sides, her hair was shorter than when they had last seen her. Her strong features were arranged in a grin as she shook her head at her partner's antics and stepped past the tangle of friends at play to approach the bar.

The final one to ascend was Cara, who Cali had met on the night of the battle at the docks against the Kraken. Diana's second in command seemed as capable as her boss. She wore an almost identical outfit and held a matching carryall. Their prowess made her feel self-conscious like she was an amateur playing at a sport they were pros at.

But they're not matriarchs of a noble house, I bet, so that's something. She rolled her eyes inwardly at her nonsense. "Hi, Diana, Cara. Thank you for coming."

Diana dropped her heavy bag on the floor and slid onto

the chair beside her with a relaxed laugh. "Well, when Nylotte tells you to do something, it's generally best to do it, I've discovered."

"Right?" She had arrived independently at the same conclusion. "She's like a force of nature."

The other agent took the seat next to her boss. "Most definitely. But she has more knowledge than anyone else I've ever met. We're lucky she's willing to teach us."

"So," Diana said briskly, "she said you need a lift to Paris and maybe support once we get there but wouldn't say more. Because, you know, *Nylotte*." The emphasis on the last word perfectly encapsulated the Drow's often maddening games and made all three of them laugh again.

Cali nodded. "There's a museum, and somewhere inside it is a piece of a sword. It's most likely one of the shards of my family's heirloom weapon, which I need to reconstruct." She didn't feel ready to share the situation about Atreo so she didn't explain the reason behind the search. "So, getting us there and helping me make sure nothing nasty is waiting would be awesome. My enemies tried to trap me with another blade fragment recently, and while I don't think they have anything to do with this one, it would be better to be safe rather than sorry."

The agent tapped her finger on the table. "How did the sword wind up broken?"

She shrugged. "That's unclear. All I know is that it's in several pieces and my parents were looking for them. I can only assume an opposing house either broke it or took advantage of the situation to scatter the parts as a way to make life difficult for my family."

"How many do you have?" Cara asked.

"A couple, at least, with a line on a couple more. My parents apparently collected extra fragments, and a friend of Nylotte's is working on finding out exactly what's there and what's still needed. He thinks we're missing four plus the pommel."

Tanyith entered the conversation abruptly. "But we have the location of two and have a fairly solid hope that we'll be able to find the rest. The last one was in a cave on Oriceran." He sounded more hopeful and positive than he had in weeks.

Diana nodded. "So, tell me about your enemies."

Cali laughed. "Where do I begin? Up here, the Zatoras —a human crime syndicate—don't particularly like us. Or anyone, for that matter. They recently attacked the leader of the magical council for no apparent reason. On the other side are the Atlanteans, who have a well-established gang, multiple street drugs that are in heavy demand, and try to kill me repeatedly by means of Atlantean ritual combat."

Zeb growled his annoyance. "Fortunately, they've not proven adequate to that task. Far from it, really."

She nodded. "Then we have the New Atlantis folks. The Malniets are the ones who were responsible for the Kraken and were behind the attack that forced my parents to flee. I have them wrapped up in a ritual challenge too, but it won't solve the problem because the process moves too slowly. I'm looking for another option. Plus, I've been told I can't trust any of the remaining seven noble houses either, although only one—Cormier—has taken any clear steps."

Tanyith added, "Don't forget the Empress."

Cali chuckled. "Oh, and yeah, Empress Shenni claims to be my friend but her family betrayed mine. I don't have even a smidgeon of trust for her in my heart."

Cara shook her head. "We're well acquainted with untrustworthy folks too. Sometimes, the only way to deal with them is to put them into the ground."

Rath yelled, "Yippee Kai Yay," and leapt upward. He was briefly visible above the bar before he plummeted out of sight again.

Both Cara and Diana laughed at his antics, and the latter explained, "He's been a little cooped up at our base. He's used to having an active social life. Maybe we should send him to hang out with your companion more often."

The girl laughed. "Fyre would love that, I'm sure of it."

Like someone had flipped a switch, the agent became businesslike. "Okay, with the time difference, we have five hours or so before nightfall in Paris. We should start to plan for this adventure."

The rest of the morning and early afternoon was spent studying floor plans, looking at the pictures Diana's techs had managed to dig up, and watching a feed on a heavy-duty laptop Cara had brought. It was from the building's security systems as they closed for the night. The agents had unpacked their bags and donned their tactical gear, which made them look like warriors. Even Rath had his smaller-sized version of the gear. Cali was amused to see that his weapon of choice seemed to be combat batons, very similar to her sticks.

We're kindred spirits.

She and Tanyith had portaled to the bunker to equip and returned to find Diana deep in conversation with someone. Cara handed them comm units and after she'd snugged it into her ear, she heard the discussion. The lead agent asked, "What do you mean, they're tagged?"

A woman's voice, simultaneously businesslike and sarcastic, replied, "Tagged. You know. Wearing a tag. Honestly, why are you such a Luddite?"

"Right, Glam," Diana countered, "you're smarter than everyone. Let's pretend you've already proven that yet again and get to the part where you explain what the hell you mean, shall we?"

Cali heard the amusement in both the voices on the channel and thought that if she was ever in charge of people, she'd want that kind of relationship with them. Cara leaned closer and whispered, "Glam is our head tech."

"Right, boss, sure." The sound of keyboarding was faintly audible behind the tech's words. "So, the museum has impressive security systems but it appears they're all keyed to ID tags. If you're wearing one, the systems more or less ignore you. What this means is that there might be a number of people inside, but if we can't see them on cameras, none of the other sensors will report them because of the tags."

Diana frowned. "Can we spoof them?"

"Not without one to use as a template. Copying wouldn't be tough, although you don't have the right gear for it."

The agent turned to face her. "So, do we need to be subtle here? Or is this basically a smash and grab?"

"It's totally a smash and grab."

She grinned. "Good, I like it simple." Her eyes defocused as she spoke to the tech. "So, the plan is to get in, get what we need, and get out. In that case, the only reason to worry about the tags is that they might be hiding op forces, correct?"

"You got it, boss."

"Okay. We can deal with that. Is your co-troublemaker ready to handle alarms and stuff?"

A male voice entered the conversation. "Hey. I resent that remark. I am the main troublemaker. She's the co-troublemaker."

Glam snorted. "Please, Deacon. You don't even approach my level of proficiency."

Diana rolled her eyes at Cali and replied, "Okay. Good. Talk to you from France." She studied both Cali and Tanyith and said, "Nice gear but kind of basic. We probably have toys you could use."

They exchanged glances and shook their heads. Cali replied, "At this point, we'd only be confused. I wouldn't say no to the chance to train with you sometime, though. I'm fundamentally a fan of toys to use against criminals."

The agents both chuckled. "Consider it done. You're both invited— Fyre and Zeb too if he's willing to leave the bar for a while. Does he actually live here?"

She laughed. "No, it only seems like it."

"Good, then. Bring him along." She turned to Cara. "Are you ready?" The other woman nodded. Diana called, "Rath, knock it off and get the rest of your gear on." The troll raced to the basement, where the agents had left their equipment, with the Draksa nipping at his heels.

Cali shook her head. "This will be interesting."

The woman laughed. "My friend, you have no idea. Every day with Rath is an adventure, and I can only assume your buddy Fyre will make him worse."

CHAPTER NINETEEN

The portal deposited them a few blocks away from their target, and the agents immediately led the way to the rooftops. Diana was in constant communication with the techs, and to judge by the conversation, the glasses she, Cara, and Rath wore were somehow computerized and displayed data. She was instantly envious and thought how handy such a tool would have been in the dark hospital.

Well, maybe when this is over, I can ask for one. Since they work for the government, they're probably only a billion dollars each or something.

She crouched beside the others at the edge of the building and peered over an ornamental wall that ran around the perimeter. This part of Paris was beautiful, with glittering lights everywhere and a surprising number of people out on the streets. The area in front of the museum was grassy and separated from the sidewalk by a set of high hedges, which she thought would give them the opportunity to get over the street and down to ground level without being seen. Security personnel were in evidence, but they didn't look particularly concerned about anything other than the conversations they were engaged in.

"It seems like a nice vacation spot," she whispered to Tanyith. "You know, if vacations were possible for any of us."

He nodded and laughed. "Someday, maybe. Although you'll probably have to spend all yours in New Atlantis."

Cali groaned. "Which is so not a vacation paradise. What with the random attacks and the endless politicking, no thanks."

Diana's voice jerked them away from their conversation. "Wait, Deacon. I have eyes on some type of motion inside the building. It shows on thermal. Do you see it on the security system?"

His response came back almost instantly and sounded distinctly irritated. "No. And what's worse, I don't have it on the sensors or the cameras."

"So. They're hiding behind illusion and they have one of Glam's all-powerful tags?"

"That would be my assessment."

She was silent for a couple of moments, then said, "I only see one. But that doesn't make much sense."

"It could be that someone screwed their illusion up," Cara suggested. "It might simply be dumb luck."

Diana turned to face Cali. "This is almost certainly a trap. There are probably people in there with access to magic, at least. For all we know, there are others in cool suits that hide them from our thermals and with tags that keep them off the sensors positioned outside the range of the cameras. That's not a reason for us not to go, but if you think there's an option to reach your goal that might be safer, now's the time to say so."

The girl shook her head. "I need the pieces and this reinforces the likelihood that one is inside."

"How do you think they knew we were coming tonight?" Tanyith asked. "Or are they camping out waiting for us?"

She shrugged. "They could have someone in the library, I guess, and heard me talking to Scoppic. But if it's one of the Nine, they surely have the resources to have guarded it since the moment I came onto the scene. I don't think there's a way to be sure."

"You should probably do a full security audit when you get home, though," Cara added. "We can help. Rath is particularly good at that." The troll nodded. He looked very serious in his earphones, body armor, goggles, and weapons, with a strange rectangular box on his back. The smile showed that it was still him beneath, however.

Diana had made final plans with the techs and finally fell silent. "Okay, last gear check." She and Cara made sure the other's straps were tightened before each checked to be sure their pistols and blades were ready to be drawn. The handle of a sword protruded over the leader's shoulder and her second in command carried long daggers in thigh sheaths. Both had thinner than usual bulletproof vests with magazines for their weapons slotted into small pockets, a few of them with blue stripes on them. Potions and more magazines were located in other places as well.

Basically, they're walking arsenals. Even Rath, with his batons and potions, looked entirely ready to rumble.

Tanyith leaned closer and whispered loudly, "We need better stuff."

She laughed. "Right?"

Diana chuckled and added, "We can help you there. But now, it's time to put your game faces on. Let's get to it."

The two agents went first and launched themselves high with bursts of magic to land cleanly on the grass in front of the museum. They paused and waited to see if the guards near the entrance would react, but the men continued to talk and smoke, oblivious to the action around them.

Tanyith followed, and he touched down cleanly as well. Fyre and Rath leapt off the building together and the Draksa spread his wings wide to glide across the distance. A set of mechanical wings snapped out of the box on the troll's back, and he flew in formation with Fyre. Cali had volunteered to go last since her landings weren't usually as clean as those who could use telekinesis to assist them. Diana had promised to assist but they'd all concurred it would be best if everyone else was in position first.

She blasted herself off the roof and the other woman's magic wound around her and guided her cleanly to the ground. Cali shook her head. "Damn, I have to figure out how to do that for myself." It was by far the least dramatic landing she'd ever managed. The two other women and the troll had already begun to advance toward the entrance, and she and her partners followed a few steps behind.

When they were close, Diana whispered, "Everyone, hold. Cara, you have the one on the left. The other's mine."

Both women drew the pistols on their left hips, which Cali only belatedly realized were different than the ones in their shoulder holsters.

Simultaneous snapping sounds broke the quiet, and both guards fell. The agents ran forward and trussed them quickly with black zip-ties, tossed their weapons away, and hid their still forms between the greenery and the wide stone porch they'd stood on.

"What did you do to them?" Cali asked.

Cara grinned as she returned to their side. "Stun guns. Kind of like a taser but better."

"Oh, damn, I need one of those."

The agents laughed, and Rath said, "Where does he get all those wonderful toys?"

She turned to him and asked, "The Joker?"

He smiled and did a backflip. "I'm Batman."

Diana sighed. "Save the movie quotes for later, Rath. We'll go in the main doors here. Remember, there is a balcony above us. Fyre, Rath, that's yours. When we change rooms, if there's no access, you come down and head up again." Both magical creatures nodded. "Tanyith, Cali, you're our rear guard. We'll advance two by two. If we get into a tussle, any newcomers from the back belong to you and any reinforcements from the front are ours. The techs say our target is most likely in the basement, so keep your eyes open while we move through but try not to get distracted. We go fast, and once we have it, we portal out. Got it?"

They both nodded and Cali said, "Thank you for this."

The agent grinned. "Hell, we're glad for the opportunity. It's been too damn slow lately."

Cara snorted. "Amen to that. So, let's go kick ass, shall we?"

They advanced out of the entry chamber with its admissions desk in the center and arched accesses on both sides and stepped into the first room. The skeletons of smaller dinosaurs filled it to create an oval shape with a straight corridor down the middle and a curved path on either side. Deacon spoke calmly over the comms. "There are no visible enemies in this room. One guard is in the next and walking away from you."

Rath fired a hook of some kind from a launcher attached to his forearm and was winched up to the balcony on the left, and Fyre flew up to the one on the opposite side. Even though everything appeared peaceful, a shiver of anticipation ran down her back.

"Clear up here," the troll said.

Fyre sent confidence to her, and she announced, "Fyre says the same."

"Forward, then," Diana replied. Ahead of them was an entry into what seemed to be a room three times as long as the one they were in. The two on the balconies descended and they all crossed the threshold together. Cali gazed in appreciation at the huge Tyrannosaurus Rex skeleton that towered above her. The head was several times the size of the Draksa, and the rest of the body was equally impressive.

Cara announced, "Clear left," from the side of the room she was on, and the young woman expected to hear the agents' leader say the same.

Instead, she froze. "Illusions present. My detection bracelet is freezing."

Cali had no idea what the second part of the statement meant but the first part was obvious. It became even more so when huge steel doors dropped to cut off their escape from the back.

"Cover—now," Diana snapped, and everyone blurred into motion.

The reaction was not an instant too soon, as a ball of fire flashed through the space where they had stood and pounded against the far wall. It spent its force on the metal of the barrier and the marble of the walls but fortunately didn't set anything alight

"What do we have?" Cara yelled,

Rath replied quickly. "Two here, heading in now." Fyre roared and belched frost at a target on the upper level of the other side of the room.

Diana said, "I see six thermals on ground level in this room. Two on your side, four over here." She must have heard something Cali didn't, because she responded authoritatively. "I don't give a damn if they've cut access off from outside. Get back into the system and make sure the doors to our objective are clear."

Cara darted out from her position on the left and charged toward the two at that side of the room. Cali located another taking aim at her and fired a force blast across the span between them to knock them down and out of sight. She raced to the left to support Cara, and her mouth dropped open in fear as one of the people the other woman had targeted launched a line of shadow that the agent made no attempt to dodge. Instinctively, she poured magic into her muscles. She knew she couldn't get there in time to stop the bolt but hoped she could at least make sure a second didn't follow.

When the bolt arrived, she was two feet behind Cara, close enough to hear a loud snap followed by a cracking sound. The impact didn't stop the other woman, who ran forward and vaulted into a kick that pistoned the side of her foot into the magical's jaw. The power of the blow combined with the momentum of her run shattered bone and hurled her target away. She landed perfectly in balance and delivered a spinning kick to the other one as Cali's force bolt struck him. He spun wildly to impact with a tall column and fell bonelessly to the floor.

The agent grinned at her. "Nice one."

Sounds of fighting to her right made her turn quickly, but the three enemies who were still up summoned a wall of force and fled deeper into the museum. Another sprawled awkwardly and looked severely injured.

Holy hell. One fight, and the body count is higher than in my whole life. These people don't kid around.

CHAPTER TWENTY

"Let's get after them," Diana ordered. "Cara, switch to the expensive stuff." The second in command drew her pistol, ejected the magazine, and swapped it for one with blue stripes from her vest.

Cali stepped beside her and asked, "What's that about?"

The woman grinned. "Anti-magic bullets. They cost entirely too much money but are perfect against magicals, at least until they realize what they're up against and adapt their tactics."

A shiver went through her at the thought of the wicked rounds the Zatoras sometimes carried. "I'm glad you all are on our side."

Cara nodded. "The enemies we face are powerful. We need every edge we can get."

Diana interrupted their conversation. "Cara, since you have a cracked deflector, I'll take point. You're second, followed by Cali and Tanyith. Rath and Fyre, you stay in the middle on the flanks. Trust physical cover first, then magical protection. You never know what they're packing."

She strode forward to the lead position and everyone followed as ordered. Cali obeyed without thought, such was the authority the woman radiated.

In their earpieces, Deacon said, "I have surveillance up. Cameras show magicals and armored troops in the next room. The stairs to the basement are after that."

A new voice Cali didn't recognize added, "Boss, you should be alert for explosives. There are suspicious-looking boxes on the video. They could be nothing or could be something. I'd double-box and crush them to be sure."

Diana paused in her advance and the others stopped. "Where?"

"At the head of the stairs—both sets—and at the landing."

"Okay. Thanks, Khan. Glam, Deacon, find us another way in case their plan is to collapse the whole staircase. Even if we have to blow a hole in the floor or something." The agent moved forward and they all fell into step again. When they reached the far side of the chamber, she stopped and pointed. "Two thermals left and two right. There might be troops in chill suits above us or anywhere else in the room." None were in their line of sight but it made sense that they'd wait until they had the element of surprise. Of course, whoever it was hadn't anticipated the agents' tech.

That thought sent Cali's mind off on a tangent. *That's a good question, actually. Who's doing this? It seems a little big to be the Atlantean gang.*

"If we can capture one to learn who they are," she whispered, "that would probably be useful."

168

"That's standard procedure," Cara replied, "but only if it's possible to do it safely."

Diana cut them off. "Going in three, two, one, go." She raced forward into the room, her pistol extended in front of her, and swept the weapon to cover the right-hand side. Cara did the same on the other side, while Cali summoned a shield in place of her left stick and held the other ready. Tanyith had chosen only magic and had a shield in his off hand. Rath's batons were already drawn and Fyre stalked low to the ground, ready to make a serpentine charge when an enemy was sighted.

The next chamber was modeled after a prehistoric forest and trees covered most of the floor. Paths snaked through them and more skeletons of every size were dotted around. If Cali had planned an ambush, she would have held off until her quarry had reached this room.

I guess it's good they were overexcited. Gunshots sounded, seemingly from everywhere in front of them, and she dove for cover behind one of the trunks. Tanyith did the same in the other direction. The agents all reacted differently.

Rath shouted, "I am the law," and barreled toward the far-left corner of the room. He grew larger with each step and by the time he reached his destination, he topped seven feet. His equipment was scattered on the ground along his path, apparently designed to fall free.

Fyre will be full of envy over that ability. She imagined a seven-foot Draksa fighting her for the blankets on her bed and was thankful he couldn't do it.

Cara and Diana had holstered their pistols and drew the stun guns. They fired almost simultaneously but their targets didn't drop. The second in command growled with irritation. "Electrical dispersion tech. They must have cost a pretty penny."

The leader drew her pistol with a curse. "Bryant is gonna be ticked that we wasted anti-magic bullets on humans." She squeezed several rounds off and one of the troopers fell.

Amusement was evident in Cara's teasing tone, which seemed like a mismatch to the situation. "Well, I'm sure you can find a way to distract him, boss. Take one for the team. Hell, take two." More pistol fire punctuated the words and another enemy collapsed.

"I'm cheap, but not that cheap," Diana replied. Her voice reverted to all business as she commanded, "Hold fire." The Draksa swooped across the line of enemy troops and blasted them with frost to ice the entire group. The enemies didn't react to him, which was both a sign of his prowess and a benefit of having two sharpshooters for them to focus on.

Cali climbed carefully out of cover. "So, this is simply a normal day for you all, is it?"

Cara laughed. "Basically, yeah." She and Diana both ejected the used magazines and slotted in new ones as if it was an automatic action once the room was clear.

"So, we'll stay back here and provide emotional support." Tanyith sounded impressed. "I think y'all have this covered."

Diana waved everyone forward and walked toward the staircases in the room beyond. "We have better tech than most mercenaries—which is no doubt what these are—plus magic. It's an uneven fight unless they have anti-magic bullets or magical assistance. We won't have nearly as great an advantage when we get to the real resistance."

The younger woman frowned. "Wait, that wasn't real?"

"They're testing. While they'd surely have been happy if these had eliminated us, there's no way they would have counted on it. No, we'll face a mixed force at some point and that will be the real battle."

"I am so glad you decided to come along."

The agents laughed and Rath stepped beside them at his normal size again. He finished putting his equipment on, and Cara checked it to be sure everything was right before she gave him a thumbs-up.

"I can do this all day," he observed, and Diana shook her head and replied, "No more Marvel movies for you, buddy."

They strode into the room with the staircases. A statue stood between them—some kind of Neanderthal humanoid, Cali guessed—and marble stairs descended on both sides. As the Khan person had warned, small boxes were placed at the ends of each, four of them in the room.

"Claymores, you think?" Cara asked.

Diana shrugged. "Maybe. Or something to turn stone into shrapnel. Either way, it sucks." She turned to face them. "Okay, New Orleans people, it's time to earn your pay." Her smile ensured they knew it was a joke. "Cara will create an inner box around the one on the left, and I'll do an outer box. When those are in place, she'll crush it with hers and mine will contain whatever surprise waits within. At least, that's the plan."

Her teammate took advantage of the pause. "And the

boss's plans always, always work out exactly as she intends them to."

The other woman extended a single finger at her subordinate and continued to speak. "Tanyith, put a wall up to separate it from us and from the other boxes. Cali, wrap the closest box in its own shield in case everything else fails. We don't want these things to chain-trigger one another. Rath and Fyre, find cover."

No one argued. Cali released her magic and imagined a square of force twice as large as the suspicious box and wrapped it. Tension filled her as she slipped the magic between the bottom and the floor, but the device didn't detonate and she exhaled a long, relieved breath.

Heh. They're probably not explosives at all and this is a waste of time.

"Is everyone ready?" Cara asked. Affirmative replies followed. "Okay, here we go."

She made no visible effort, but the effect was dramatic. A loud muffled bang was immediately followed by fire and smoke that filled Diana's shield. It died quickly without the oxygen to burn. The lead agent said, "Ow. That was some pushback."

Cara nodded. "It's powerful stuff. They definitely wanted to collapse the stairs and us, preferably in pieces."

"You have some troublesome enemies, Matriarch," Diana stated.

"That I do." Cali shook her head. "I'm not sure I'll be able to repay this particular favor anytime soon."

The woman pointed at the next box. "Same plan, people." As they applied their magics, she added, "No compensation is necessary other than being our intel source on New Atlantis. With your connections and influence there, that will benefit our work considerably."

She snorted and whispered theatrically, "Did you hear that, Tanyith? I have connections and influence. And here I thought I was little more than comic relief with a target painted on my back."

"Why not both?" he replied and soft laughter filtered across the channel.

They detonated the remaining explosives at the top of the stairs and those on the landing without incident. The delay was frustrating, but there was no question that it was the only way to handle the situation. Finally, they reached the bottom floor.

Deacon's voice came as a sudden intrusion over the comm. "They're waiting for you two rooms ahead so there are probably more surprises between here and there. We haven't been able to identify any as the cameras and sensors have been physically disassociated."

Cali frowned. "What now?"

Cara laughed. "Ripped out. Deacon likes fancy words."

"I like accurate words," he countered. "Unlike you uncivilized cretins."

The second in command laughed. "Glam, smack him for me, please."

Diana shook her head but a smile spread across her face. "Okay, Rath, Cara. Let's do flash-bangs and go in and mop up. Cara left, me center, and short stuff, you have right." The trio moved into position near the archway that led to the next room. "Grenade out."

Each threw two grenades quickly before Rath's batons snicked open and the women drew pistols. Loud crashes sounded ahead, along with shouts and at least one scream of pain. The agents surged into the room and the others followed. Pistols barked, and figures fell. A fireball careened toward Cali. She conjured a shield, blocked it, and summoned her sticks. Without slowing, she caught a force bolt on one and grounded a lightning attack with the other as she sprinted forward in the direction of the two magicals in the front left corner of the room.

Shadow bolts streaked over her shoulders as Tanyith followed, and her foes were forced to drop their attacks in order to defend themselves. She targeted the one closest to the wall and fired force blasts to keep him on the defensive until she moved within range. He had created a full-body shield similar to the ones she favored, so she drove a force bolt into the wall behind him. Shards erupted from the impact, sliced him, and distracted him enough that he moved the shield and provided an opening. She hammered his forearm with her stick and shattered it, and when he lost his focus from the shock, she felled him with a quick triple-strike to his head.

Tanyith had borrowed a page from her book and bull-dozed bodily into the other one, who currently slid down the wall and left a trail of scarlet from where her head had struck it. Cali dimly realized that there were conversations going on and tuned in to hear Cara say, "Clear here," and Rath reply, "Here, too."

"Uh, clear here," she stammered. "Two magicals down."

Gunfire sounded from the chamber beyond and a concerted barrage of bullets flew through the arched doorway. Diana yelled, "Cover," and everyone obeyed. She asked, "Deacon, confirm that our objective is in the next room?"

He replied instantly. "As far as we know, boss. It seems likely. There are several safes in there, bigger than those we use for rifles. If I secured something valuable, that's where I'd put it."

"Okay, it's time to wrap this up. Everyone, reload and get ready. We go on the count of ten."

CHAPTER TWENTY-ONE

The agents repeated the process they had used in the previous room and lobbed grenades prior to their advance. Like Diana had said, though, the enemy had gathered information as they made their way through the museum and had shielded against the barrage of light and sound.

Gunfire greeted Cali as she raced into the chamber and she cringed under the cover of her force shield and said a small prayer that the mercenaries didn't have anti-magic bullets. When the rounds rebounded harmlessly, she sent thanks to the universe and chose one of the rifle wielders. A blast of force flung him into the wall behind him and he fell senseless.

Fyre flashed in front of her and took the brunt of a lightning attack she hadn't detected. He screamed in anger but she felt no sensations of pain coming from him. She turned to the new opponent but he was engulfed in the swirl of smoke and action. Tanyith traded punches with a mercenary a few feet away from her, and she skipped in and caught the woman with a sidekick in the ribs. His uppercut took her out of the fight, and her helmet made a sharp sound as it thumped against the floor.

They separated to seek new enemies. She crossed behind Diana, who calmly fired bullets into magicals and non-magicals alike while her second in command protected her from counterattacks. The two operated almost as a single individual in the way they moved and attacked. When Cali stepped through a waft of smoke, she discovered Rath delivering a wicked series of blows with his batons to a magical who'd obviously failed to stop him from closing. She noticed the dark crystals on the front of his vest and realized that they were almost certainly magic protection based on what Diana had said earlier. It made sense, and she filed the knowledge away to ask about later. Perhaps the stones might provide the edge Ikehara needed to even the odds in a magical battle.

Instinctively, she raised her sticks in an X to catch the huge overlapping cones of fire two mages unleashed at her. She threw one stick at the enemy on the right to distract him, then lunged toward the one on the left and made sure to position him in the other one's line of sight. Her mind reached to Fyre's with a request that he take the second one, and affirmation bounced back.

Meanwhile, the one in front of her had cast lightning and when she blocked it, launched a punch at her. The unexpected attack was too fast for her hasty shield to catch it and landed on her right shoulder. The arm felt nothing but pain for a long instant before it became numb and refused to respond. She realized her foe's fist was wreathed in lightning as it swung again.

That's new. A corner of her mind considered how she might use such a physical-magical combo while the rest reacted to the attack. She stepped with her right foot and he made the mistake of overextending to try to reach her. Instantly, she dropped her left-hand stick and stretched to grasp his wrist to use it as a lever to pull him in a different direction. Faced with the choice of letting it break or throwing himself down, her foe chose the latter and she powered a boot into his temple. He moaned and rocked his head so she kicked him in the ribs to keep him out of the fight. While it was tempting, she didn't want to risk another blow to his brain.

Something drove into her from behind and hurled her forward and down. She barely managed to position her uninjured arm to protect herself, then twisted with a curse at her dysfunctional limb when it failed to assist. Rath was on top of her, and the wall to her right was on fire.

He grinned. "Remember the five rules of dodgeball. Dodge, duck, dip, dive, and dodge." In the next moment, he was up and running again and she stared after him and shook her head.

Suddenly, the surrounding noise ceased and everyone called, "Clear," in turn. She groaned as she scrambled to her feet and joined the others in the center of the room.

Diana looked at her hanging arm and grinned. "Not bad for that fight. Lightning punch?" She nodded. "I thought that's what I saw. It should come back in a few minutes or you can take a healing potion. The magic overloads the nerves." The others had scrapes and cuts, and Cara had a bruise on her cheek that had already begun to darken.

"I'll watch the stairs," Tanyith said and walked to that side of the room.

The lead agent nodded. "Cara, you deal with the safe. I'll keep an eye on the other side. Rath, Fyre, you're the second line of defense." They spread out and Cali walked to Cara.

"So, what's the plan?"

The other woman held up a rectangular box with flickering lights on the front. "We let our techs take care of it." She placed it on one of the giant old-fashioned safes above the combination wheel. The container was seven feet tall and about half that wide and deep. Several of them were present in the room. She spun the knob slowly and talked to the techs, who told her when to stop and move in the opposite direction. The first and second safes didn't hold the shard, but when the third one opened, it was immediately visible. The agent stepped aside and Cali retrieved the heavy fabric she'd brought and wrapped it securely.

"Are we good?" Diana asked.

She breathed deeply. "We're good."

"Cool. Let's blow this popsicle stand."

Cara muttered something that resulted in her boss backhanding her across the chest, and they both laughed. Cali opened a portal to the basement of the Dragons and they all stepped through together.

They changed into civilian clothes before they ascended to the main room of the tavern. The place was incredibly busy and Zeb shooed the people seated at the bar to make space for them. In short order, they had ciders of varying potency, bread, and bowls of stew in front of them, except for Fyre. The Draksa had his stew behind the bar but with water to drink. They ate and chatted about random things before everyone accepted another helping and continued to do the same.

Finally, when she was stuffed and could eat no more, Cali withdrew the fabric-covered shard and set it on the wooden surface in front of her. Zeb inclined his chin toward it. "Is it what you thought it was?"

She shrugged. "Only Alessand will know for sure." She unwrapped it carefully to reveal the silver metal with its deep engravings. "But it looks right."

"So what's your next move?" Diana asked.

"First, I'll deliver this to Stonesreach. But after that, once it's safe, I need to find out who set the trap so I can be sure to reward them appropriately."

Cara laughed. "Now that is a good attitude."

Rath stood on his stool and began to pull items out of a pouch he wore on his belt. "Always another way."

Diana frowned. "No out of context Matrix quotes. Especially from the sequels."

The troll stuck his tongue out at her and continued to unpack things onto the bar. When he was finished, he pushed the stack toward her and the two agents nudged it the rest of the way.

"What is this?" she asked.

He shrugged. "Found it."

Diana laughed. "Rath is rather like a crow. He likes shiny things and likes them even more when they belonged

TR CAMERON

to criminals." He nodded with a grin and turned to his food again.

Cali rifled through the items until she noticed something notable. "Hey, Tay, does that look like what I think it does?"

He nodded. "It sure does."

She grinned and held the badge up, which had probably been attached to a necklace or a belt buckle. "This is the symbol of one of the nine noble houses of New Atlantis." She pulled her necklace out. "This compass is the sigil of House Leblanc, for instance. Each of them has one."

Tanyith continued, "And this nasty looking hook is the marker for the family that tried to destroy Cali's house before and who she has to defeat in order to...uh, resolve issues in New Atlantis."

She was glad he hadn't mentioned her brother. Even though she didn't think anything bad would come from it, she also didn't want the agents to look at her with sympathy. "House Malniet. Bastards one and all."

Diana nodded. "Well, good. That's one question solved. So what will you do about it?"

Cali grinned. "I'll return it, of course. In the most painful way I can think of."

Cara laughed. "Right on, sister." She turned to Diana. "Boss, I think we should head back. There's no telling what trouble Glam and Deacon will get up to without your wise leadership."

The other woman rolled her eyes but rose to her feet. "You're not wrong." She extended a fist and bumped with Cali and Tanyith, and both Cara and Rath did the same. "I'll be in touch to arrange some training together." Each stopped to give Fyre a pat before they wandered down the stairs.

Zeb shook his head. "Interesting friends you have."

She laughed. "Starting with you."

"That's no way to talk to your boss."

She raised an eyebrow and folded her arms. "Based on the way Cara talks to Diana, I think it's fair to say I've been way too easy on you."

"Or that Diana's too easy on her," he retorted. "A mistake I surely won't make."

Tanyith shook his head and laughed. "Anyway, it's good to win. Relationship work and plotting against the other houses can wait until tomorrow." He yawned and stretched. "I'm off to bed."

Cali nodded. "Rest up. Tomorrow, we'll travel to New Atlantis and decide out how best to shove this down Styrris Malniet's throat."

CHAPTER TWENTY-TWO

The request from Diana to join her in New Atlantis had been a welcome surprise. Cali, Tanyith, Fyre, and the agent all stepped through from the basement of the tavern to her home in the underwater city in the early afternoon of the next day.

Jenkins welcomed them instantly, and Emalia appeared a few moments later, descending from the second floor in a set of formal robes her great niece hadn't seen before. They were in the colors of House Leblanc, a deep red sheath under a turquoise wrap that extended almost to her feet on her left side. "Do you have a date?" she asked the older woman.

Her great aunt laughed. "Yes. With the Empress."

Diana whistled and Cali made the appropriate introductions before they headed to the big table in the kitchen and the nearby coffeemaker. The agent again carried a heavy pack and placed it beside her chair as she sat. They shared small talk while the coffee brewed, and Emalia busied herself gathering crackers and cheese, plus fruit from Oriceran she'd bought from a local market. The berries tasted like a blend of pineapple and orange, with a sour finish that made Cali's jaw hurt. She loved them instantly.

"So, why are you visiting the Empress?" Diana asked.

Emalia shrugged and took a sip of her coffee. Cali considered the fact that she'd enticed the woman to occasionally switch from tea a personal victory. "It's time we were reacquainted. I knew her when she was young but not since she became monarch."

Her niece hurried to add, "She's my spy in New Atlantis. It's an information-gathering effort. We don't have any sources in the palace so our approach needs to be a little bolder."

Diana nodded. "It makes sense. And on that topic, I brought presents." She unzipped the pack and retrieved a rectangular gray plastic box. Once she'd spun it to face Cali, she pulled the top back to reveal a set of eight tiny wires with buds on the end and sixteen small black boxes.

"Oooh, gifts. I love gifts." Fyre snorted his agreement from under the table, and she rubbed him with her foot. "What are they?"

"Listening devices, recorders, and receivers. The entire network is self-contained and self-powered, so it should work here without a problem. Put the wire in the place where you want to listen and the recorder somewhere nearby. It doesn't need to be too close. The microphone stays inactive until it hears something, then streams the data to the recorder in short, unpredictable bursts. Glam tells me there's no way anyone would detect a pattern. The connection between the recorder and receiver works the same. It's useless for real-time information but perfect for avoiding detection over a long-term surveillance period."

Tanyith grinned. "Nice," he said and picked one of the wires up. It was no longer than the top joint of his index finger, and the bud was barely larger than the thin line that trailed from it.

"Is there a way to detect these magically?" Emalia frowned.

Diana shrugged. "Anything's possible, of course, but we haven't managed it—and we have very skilled magicals working for us. Even Nylotte wasn't able to find the one I hid in her shop."

Cali laughed. "You're braver than I thought."

The other woman nodded. "Sometimes, I need to win one with her."

I totally feel that. "Thank you. I think one in the palace, one in Jehenel, and one in the Malniet mansion to start with if we can get one in there."

Emalia and Tanyith nodded, and Diana closed the box and pushed it to her. "Next, Cara guessed you might be able to use these." She slid two holsters across the table. Each held one of the strangely shaped stun guns the agents had used the day before. Cali pulled one out and examined it.

"It looks like a Phaser from *Star Trek* or a blaster from *Star Wars* or another *Star* something."

The agent laughed. "It really does. Our techs are science fiction fans so I'm sure it's deliberate. But they work well." She produced another two small rectangles and a box. "Here are spare cartridges and a charger. The stun pistols should give you an edge if you're being sneaky."

TR CAMERON

Cali nodded. Even though she wasn't all that comfortable with guns for anything other than stealing them from the enemy and selling them, the nonlethal ones appealed to her. "Again, thank you."

Diana dipped into the bag and retrieved another case, this one about a foot wide and three-quarters of that long, but shallow. She opened it to display the crystals Rath had worn the day before. "These are magic deflectors, although absorbers might be a better word. They create a field that defeats magic. They're essentially flawless but they can only absorb a certain amount before they crack. We all have them woven into our gear. These are for you to use as you see fit."

Cali nodded slowly. "I think I've heard of these before."

"You have," Tanyith interjected, "from Kendra, if nowhere else. AET forces use them. They're hard to come by, though."

The agent chuckled. "They are. But we have a hookup. Even so, it's not an unlimited supply. Use them wisely."

"I literally can't thank you enough."

"You don't need to. You're fighting the same fight we are, only in a different arena. That makes us teammates."

She grinned. "Okay. But I owe you."

Diana nodded. "That is exactly how I like it. I'm sure I'll have occasion to cash the voucher in sometime." She stood. "Now, how about you send me home? Rath and I have a knife-throwing competition later, and I need to find out how to cheat. I'm tired of losing to him."

After her visitor had left, Cali rejoined the others at the kitchen table. "She is a very nice person," Emalia commented.

"They're all nice."

"As long as you're on their side, anyway," Tanyith added. "I wouldn't want to go up against them."

She shook her head. "Me neither." The fight the day before had left no one conscious to interrogate and they hadn't been able to wait. It was only luck that the troll had snagged a clue. The agents were definitely more deadly than she ever wanted to be. With an effort, she dismissed those thoughts and turned her mind to the future.

"So, I think we let the Malniets stew for a while. The longer we don't respond, the longer they'll wonder if we know. Maybe it will keep them distracted and out of trouble for now."

Tanyith shrugged. "Sure. And when you do decide to brace them, you can finagle a way to get into the mansion to plant the bug."

Emalia nodded. "It's as good a plan as any. I agree, though, that you can't finish the ritual with them. They'll cheat and kill you before you're able to like they tried to yesterday. Because you have to retrieve the sword pieces, you're exposed."

"I know. So you need to find the rest, which means you need to play it safe at the palace. No bugs today." Cali had thought it through while she sent Diana on to her base, and as much as she wanted to get one in there, it didn't make sense for her great aunt to do it. "I'll come up with a way to get one in there. You do what you planned to do. Wrap her in words and steal all her secrets."

The older woman laughed. "You give me too much credit. This is only to ensure she knows I'm part of the game. It'll provide her something to focus on other than you when she thinks about House Leblanc."

Cali sighed. "Okay, it sounds like a plan. I'll go practice lightning. Good luck." She rose and gave Emalia a kiss on the cheek, then regarded her with a grin. "We're all counting on you in this matter of life and death. No pressure, though."

Her great aunt rolled her eyes, and the girl wandered toward the back door, laughing and with Fyre at her side.

Emalia was met in the entryway of the palace by the Empress's seneschal, who introduced herself as Gwyn. She was simply attired in a black dress with a large scarlet stripe covering the right-hand side. Her name and face conjured a memory, and she asked, "Gwyn Rivette?"

The other woman nodded with a smile and almost seemed pleased to be recognized. "Indeed. Outside the main bloodline, of course. Distant cousins. But we share the noble name if nothing else." The woman gestured and they walked deeper into the palace.

Absently, the visitor noted the rooms through which they passed and filed the information away for later. A lifetime of magical practice and instruction had given her a strong ability to attend to multiple things at once, which was invaluable at moments like these. She filled their progress with small talk and tried to plant seeds of common interest she could use later to connect with the woman.

By her deflections and subject changes, it was clear that

Gwyn was familiar with the tactic and on guard against it. That didn't bother Emalia. She'd continue to prepare the ground and if nothing grew, nothing was lost. Finally, they reached an unremarkable door.

"Please remember to show the proper respect to the Empress," the seneschal told her. "And be aware that if you should try anything inappropriate, you will be dead before you have the chance to finish it."

Emalia inclined her head and spoke with a hint of amusement. "Noted." She'd been under no illusions on that subject, in any case. One didn't become a monarch by trusting those one didn't fully control.

Gwyn opened the door and gestured for her to enter, and she stepped inside. Empress Shenni was seated behind an ornate wooden desk. The woman's clothes were gorgeous and the ruler even more so. She wore a black dress with a scarlet cape, and thick bands of hair that looked like tentacles ready to strike at her were piled atop her head, bound with a strand of pearls. Emalia walked slowly to her side and knelt to kiss her hand, then took the seat across from her at the regal gesture to do so.

A servant bustled in and filled the glasses, added one cube of ice to each, and departed. She waited until the Empress sipped, then tasted her own. It was delicious, spicy and dark. She preferred whiskey to rum but quality was quality. "It's wonderful, Empress. Thank you for the drink and for agreeing to meet me."

The woman waved an elegant hand that had rings on every finger and bracelets down her wrist. "It is nothing. I heard of your return to New Atlantis and looked forward to the chance to visit with you. I would have extended an invitation but there never seemed to be an opportunity. There is so much going on with the noble houses right now, you know."

Emalia nodded. "Indeed. Chaos and conflict are everywhere you turn."

Shenni grinned. "Exactly how I like it."

The comment made her laugh. "Well, at least you're honest."

The ruler shrugged. "Why wouldn't I be? I have my enemies, as anyone does. But while they are occupied with one another, I am free to focus my energies on the things that benefit all Atlanteans."

"Such as permitting the destruction of House Leblanc?"

Again, the Empress waved a hand dismissively. "That is distant history and very early in my reign. I had no part in that."

"But neither did you stop it."

She nodded. "Correct. That is not the role of the monarch."

Emalia smiled. "So you have no interest in the disposition of the Nine?"

Shenni grinned and revealed perfect teeth. "Oh, I wouldn't say that. Rather, I am willing to see how events play out without being directly involved."

"Are you not? Directly involved, that is? Rumors swirl about Patriarch Jehenel calling on you."

The Empress lifted her glass to her painted lips and took a sip, then set it down thoughtfully. "Come now, Emalia. We are both experienced in the ways of politics. This month it is Wymarc and next month, it will be someone else. The only way to prevent them all from turning against me is to keep them jealous of one another. Surely you too have had suitors?"

"One or two, certainly, Empress. So, let me ask plainly. Do you wish to see House Leblanc fall?"

The question appeared to catch her by surprise. *Exactly as I intended.* The woman blinked a couple of times, then answered in a neutral tone. "I have no wish to see Leblanc fall any more than I do any other of the nine houses."

Emalia nodded. *You're not as good a liar as you think, Shenni Rivette.* "Very well. Thank you for your honesty."

The Empress smiled and in it was the recognition that whatever their relationship might have been when she'd entered the room, they now occupied opposite sides of the game board.

CHAPTER TWENTY-THREE

O zahl had just finished the arduous work of replenishing his magical supplies—which involved portaling to several cities—when his Zatora phone buzzed. With a frown, he pulled it out of his pocket to see who demanded his attention, already prepared to be annoyed at Grisham for disturbing his allegedly free time.

It was Lila's number, however, and in the innocuous message were embedded code words that meant "Immediate," "Meeting," and "Club." He'd warned both of his favorite associates about contacting him for anything less than an emergency and he trusted they wouldn't act against his wishes.

So, something big is up.

He portaled to the correct street, entered the nightclub, and pushed his way through the crowd and the bouncers to ascend to the second level. When the latter objected, he gave them both a glare that sent them scurrying to their posts. He found Dalton and Lila in the same seats they'd been in the last time he'd visited, but on this occasion, they were alone with only sodas in front of them.

Another sign of trouble.

"You've checked for watchers?" he asked as he slid into the booth beside them. Lila nodded. "Both sides?"

Dalton replied in the affirmative and added, "No one from any organization is on us right now. We made sure of it."

"Okay. What's up?"

Lila answered, "Grisham plans to move tonight." She looked at her watch. "In about four hours when the Atlantean leader goes home for the night. She always takes one of three cars and one of four routes, and he plans to set up on all of them and hit any car that looks like hers."

The statement was so unlikely that it took him several seconds to process. "What the hell? Has he lost his mind? What caused this?"

The man shook his head. "We don't know and no one we trust knows. He came out of his bedroom in a frenzy and gave the orders. Everyone is scrambling now. They'll have anti-magic bullets and whatever heavy weapons he's been hiding. I think he hopes to blast the car away and be done with it. We didn't tell him or anyone other than you anything about her."

Ozahl frowned. *It's not a bad plan,* a part of his brain observed. The other parts raced through options. "Is there any reason to believe this is a one-time opportunity?"

Lila shrugged. "When we've watched her, she's been fairly consistent. I don't see any reason why it couldn't wait a day, a week—hell a month. Unless he knows something we don't."

Yeah, like his marbles are rolling away faster than he can gather them.

He shook his head. "Okay, then I guess the next question is whether this is good for the Zatoras or bad for them, and good for us or bad for us." He paused to consider the angles. While he had no desire to see Usha hurt and would do what he could to make sure that didn't occur, he didn't have an issue with Grisham making a move. In fact, it would set up what came next very well with the proper evidence planted and the appropriate story told. "I can't see a reason not to other than the fact that it's sudden. Can you?"

They exchanged glances and Dalton shrugged. "We couldn't think of one either, except that we thought you might not want it to happen."

In the most neutral voice possible, he asked, "What do you mean?"

She sighed. "Let's put our cards on the table here. You're with the Zatoras, but you're not *with* them any more than we are. Not like we are with you. They're only…a means to an end. And to be clear, we have no problem with that. We've made our choice and think you'll bring us the most success."

Dalton nodded. "Yep. What you say, goes. We don't need to know why if you don't want to share, although you're always welcome to bounce ideas off us. Working with you provides everything we want. And Grisham… well, he's clearly unpredictable."

"We don't like unpredictable," his partner added. "Unpredictable gets people killed. There's nothing wrong with seizing the moment, but this is something else entirely." She shrugged. "Tell us what you want us to do and we'll do it. Kill the woman, kill the Zatoras trying to kill the woman, whatever."

Ozahl considered them thoughtfully. Aside from Danna, he'd never had such a clear pledge of loyalty from anyone before and he discovered that he liked it.

Maybe this is what it will be like when we're a noble house. One can hope. He nodded. "We'll let it play out. Try to think of a way to get yourself assigned to one of the least likely ones, though. Grisham underestimates our enemy time and time again. Whoever does draw the short straw will find themselves with a tiger by the tail."

I'll make sure of it.

He kept the clock running in his mind. It was down to three hours, which was more than enough time to accomplish what he needed to do. He portaled to his apartment and hurried to the walk-in closet. It would require either a magician of far greater skill than his or a truly accomplished architect to detect the hidden panel at the rear of the space. He deactivated the wards and used his telekinesis to slide it aside on its concealed tracks. Behind the false wall was what he thought of as his costume shop, an array of outfits for almost any occasion.

His skill with illusion would be adequate to impersonate clothing but he liked to use what the movies called practical effects wherever possible so he could limit his use of magic to the essentials. It was less to control in his brain, which allowed him more space to deal with unexpected events. He transformed into the woman who had dined with Danna before and donned a blue suit, blouse, stockings, and heels. It was like putting on another skin as the items helped him remember to change his walk and his posture—all the things that simple illusion wouldn't take care of.

He could have sent a text to Danna but he wanted to be there in person to tell her and to give her a plausible excuse for leaving. They feared electronic interception more than the discovery of his ability to appear as several of her former partners. She'd provided him with her planned movements for the day, exactly as she always did and as he always did for her. They did their best to leave nothing to chance.

But here comes Rion Damn Bastard Bloody Grisham to mess that up royally. He shook his head in annoyance and checked his appearance in the mirror. He snagged a pair of obnoxious hoop earrings, stuck them in his earlobes, and portaled to where he guessed she'd be.

After searching the first club with growing irritation, he decided it was more likely she'd been and gone than that she'd not been there yet, so he headed to the next. It was an upscale bar that catered to the magical community and while nonmagicals were technically allowed, it was rare to see them in significant numbers. The venue had a vibe that tended to make them uncomfortable, an aura of power that set their teeth on edge as he'd heard it described.

Ozahl had been there before on several occasions, and while the bouncer didn't recognize him, the hundred-dollar bill he produced from his clutch purse and handed over was enough to get him in. The Atlantean contingent was immediately obvious—two young toughs in business suits with long, wild hair that no businessperson would ever wear. He made his way slowly across the room and made sure his stride was appropriate to his gender and his alleged status as a club-goer.

A quick stop at the bar for a drink added a cosmopolitan to go with the image, and he carried it toward the group. When he moved closer, he located Danna in a booth, chatting up one of the wealthiest wizards in town—one who felt no need to bother with politics, the council, or anything other than his own pleasure. She'd mentioned that the man was trying to get her into bed with him and also that it would never, ever happen.

The nearest guard, to his credit, tried to stop him as she approached. "Sorry, miss, this is a private gathering."

He shook his head and grinned. "I think once your boss sees me, she'll decide that she and I should have a private gathering." He added volume and flirtation to the last words, and those at the table turned to look at him. With a smile, he met Danna's gaze and extended his arms. "Darling, so good to see you again."

She stood with a broad smile and hugged him. "And you. Would you care to join us? I could introduce you to my friend here." She gestured toward the wizard.

Ozahl shook his head. "I'm afraid I only have a few minutes to spend with you before I need to be off. Perhaps your handsome companion would let me borrow you for a moment?" They'd trapped him well, and the wizard nodded magnanimously. He drew Danna to a corner and whispered, "It's tonight. Two and a half hours. In the car."

She laughed as if he'd made a joke, but her eyes were cold and hard. "Any change in plan?" They'd agreed that they would do whatever they could to keep Usha safe, as long as it didn't endanger their larger goal. He was reasonably sure that Danna would ignore the last part of the agreement if push came to shove, and it was likely that he would too.

Burning it all down by force is always an option but not a preferable one.

He nodded. "Of course not, darling." He offered her a sip of the drink, and she took it to cover his next words. "I'll need to be visible elsewhere to avoid suspicion. And she has to be in the car or we'll be outed. Have her take route three."

Danna smiled. "I have it covered. Now, come over and let me introduce you." He followed her and marveled at the way she turned the interruption into a bonus for her client, the opportunity to meet one more person he could try unsuccessfully to convince to share his bed. He waved his goodbyes a few moments later and portaled home to change again. It would require a few conversations to ensure that neither he nor his dedicated followers were present for the fight that was about to break out between the Zatoras and the Atlantean gang.

CHAPTER TWENTY-FOUR

In order to avoid revealing her inside knowledge, Danna had been forced to move less quickly than she would have liked once she extracted herself from the club. She feigned exhaustion and ordered her driver to take them to the Shark Nightclub, closed her eyes, and reclined in the leather back seat to consider how best to respond to the Zatora leader's gambit.

Avoiding it entirely wasn't an option. That would betray the existence of a source near Grisham, which absolutely needed to remain a secret until the very last moments of the game. With that off the table, precious few additional choices remained that would keep Usha safe but also give the impression that they'd been taken by surprise.

It was up to her to choose the right one and if she screwed it up, she and Usha would both likely lose their lives before the end of the night. That Ozahl would destroy Grisham and all his people immediately after provided little consolation.

By the time they pulled into the garage next door to the

club, she thought she had found a solution. The hardest part would be lying to Usha, something she'd never been all that good at. The woman had an uncanny ability to read her—and, in fact, to read anyone. It was one of the things that had made her so formidable during her rise to champion. That and her complete unwillingness to give up.

Her escorts activated the staircase that led to the underground tunnel and a few moments later, she was in the office waiting for her boss to arrive. She busied herself at the bar cart mixing two strong drinks of dark rum and pineapple juice and counted off the seconds it would take for the man she'd sent to reach the main room and convince the Atlantean leader to join her. The clock ticked in her head beneath the louder countdown to the time that Usha usually left the club.

Everything has to seem normal, even though it is anything but. She took a seat on the couch, perched on the edge of the cushion with her spine straight and her mind racing, and waited.

The other woman arrived more quickly than she'd expected. She sat across from her and took the drink, and Danna ordered, "Out," to the helper who had lingered. He shut the door softly behind him as he exited.

"Okay, what?" Usha asked. "You look like you're ready to snap."

She nodded. "Grisham's planning to kill you tonight."

The news had a visible impact. The leader lifted her drink to her lips with a slightly trembling grasp and drank half of it. After a moment, she mastered herself and dispatched whatever weakness had momentarily influenced her. "Okay. I presume we have time to plan since there's no running and screaming going on." She managed a wry smile.

Danna laughed. "Leave it to you to make a joke out of something so important. Yes, there's time to plan."

Usha shrugged. "Sometimes, things need to be put in the proper perspective. Humor helps." She frowned. "First question—when and how?"

Her leader's tone made her feel like a new recruit called upon to report. "On your drive home. They intend to hit you in the car on the way. I don't know any more than that."

"Second question—how do you know any of this?"

This was the tricky part. She needed to sell the answer so the woman would believe her. This was the only way the information would be trusted and proper precautions could be taken. She'd rehearsed it several times, but it still sounded rough in her ears. "I've cultivated a source inside their gang. I didn't want to mention it until I was sure about him and honestly, I'm still not completely positive. But acting on this material doesn't hurt us if he's wrong."

She stopped and took a sip, then gave an apologetic smile. "Sorry. I know I'm all over the place. This has me a little shaken up. Anyway, he's an addict, and it was a simple matter to have one of the girls get him hooked on Shine." The Atlanteans had several women and men willing to pretend romantic interest if it helped the gang compromise a target. "So we have him both ways—we can either cut off his supply or burn him to his boss." She cringed inwardly at so many lies but they were reasonable ones. She waited as the other woman considered her words.

Finally, Usha nodded. "Okay. You're right. Whether the

intel is correct or not doesn't matter. We should plan as if it is. But if it turns out to be good, you need to protect this source. Having someone on the inside would be invaluable."

Successfully deceiving her friend cut Danna deeply but far less than watching her die would. She exhaled in relief. "Great. Yes. Okay, so I thought we could handle it this way…"

They'd selected the most heavily armored car they owned for the run, an old Crown Victoria that had been gutted and rebuilt for strength. It guzzled gas like a drunk downed whiskey, but it was still one of the three Usha commonly used for the trip home. Each of them had tinted windows, which would work in their favor tonight.

Three guards entered the car with them. One drove while another rode shotgun, and the third sat between her and Usha in the back. Each was a proficient caster but also adept with mundane weapons. They carried rifles, which were the heaviest weapons Usha had thought they could have inside and still maintain deniability. Danna would have preferred that someone already be holding the grenade launcher stored in the trunk, but she'd had to agree it would look wrong.

Since she didn't normally ride home with Usha, a disguise was required. Her ever-present suit was gone, replaced by the standard jeans and hoodie uniform of the gang. Spikes crowned her head, her short hair arranged in a style she'd never before worn. A little makeup changed the lines of her face and made her seem heavier than her true weight, an illusion reinforced by the baggy clothes. Unless someone got close, her identity should remain undetected.

And if they do get that close, they'll have to die. It was a simple deduction and she had no problem with it. They'd known there would be casualties on the way to their goals. The only hard and fast rule was that she, Ozahl, and Usha wouldn't be among them.

The guard between them appeared nervous. He grasped and released the barrel of his rifle with his off-hand as they neared the place where the ambush would most likely occur. She hadn't received word of the final positions of the enemy forces but it didn't matter. When it came, they would be ready for it. They'd judged the likelihood highest that it would happen during the longest straight stretch of buildings on the drive since it would prevent them from being able to turn off.

"Thirty seconds until we're in the tube," the driver said,

Usha nodded. "Good. Keep your eyes open, and if you see anything at all, you gun it." After much discussion, they'd decided that their foes would expect them to stop in surprise or try to flee in reverse. The heavy body of the Crown Vic would win a collision with most other vehicles, especially if it was something that rode high like an SUV. That would be their foes' first shock. The second would be far more surprising for an opponent expecting a quick victory.

They made a turn and the driver warned them, "It could be any time now." In the next moment, they lurched forward and a loud crash behind them indicated that whatever explosive device the enemy had launched at the car had missed. Danna twisted to look over her shoulder and saw a black Escalade pull into the street behind them.

The guard in the passenger seat yelled, "Trouble," and she whipped her head around to see a matching vehicle ahead.

Her boss's voice was calm. "Okay. Stop and bail." The Crown Vic had reached the position they'd selected, where walkways into the recessed entries of the surrounding buildings would give them cover on either side. Tires squealed as they came to a halt, thrust the doors open, and sprinted into safety.

As planned, Usha and Danna turned as soon as they'd found something to hide behind and hurled fireballs at the enemies in the rear. The SUV swerved to the side to evade the magic but wasn't fast enough. The enemy vehicle caught fire and the Zatora soldiers fled. Their guard cut them down methodically with his rifle, while Usha hurled more magic at those who had launched the failed attack on the car.

Danna turned to check the front, where Zatoras fired from behind the SUV that had stopped sideways across the road. A bullet ripped through the magical shield the driver held and spun him to land heavily on the hood. The rounds that followed felled him completely.

"Anti-magic bullets," she yelled. They'd assumed the enemies would have them and had planned accordingly. The guard who'd been in the rear with them raced to the trunk, retrieved the launcher, and distributed smoke grenades in a circle around the Atlantean position. Usha, Danna, and the remaining guards flung fireballs in every direction and fell back to Usha's side. Under cover of the drifting fog and the protection of the flames, she summoned a portal and everyone else stepped through.

Danna's last act before she left was to discharge a fireball into the Crown Vic and it exploded magnificently.

Let's see how you like that, Rion Grisham, you scumbag. No evidence that we were aware in advance, only proof we're better than your people. With a wide grin, she followed the others into the portal to safety.

CHAPTER TWENTY-FIVE

When the Empress had refused to commune with her magically, Usha had immediately set out for New Atlantis. The docks at midday were filled with a bustle of activity. She surveyed the area automatically and searched for threats and for those who might want to take a shot at the champion even now, years after she'd last been in the city's limelight.

With a shake of her head, she ascended the stairs to the city. Empress Shenni's choice to meet in person wasn't unusual but it was inconvenient. It was impossible to know what Grisham was up to on the surface while she was down there. On the plus side, arguably, she'd be safe from any follow-up attacks.

From the Zatoras, anyway. She searched constantly for Caliste Leblanc, who might have discovered cause to throw the rulebook away and attack her. There was no way to tell when the information that the girl's parents had died at her hand would come out and no way to predict the result when it did. Usha had been equal parts amused and distrustful when their newest enemy had requested a meeting.

One challenge at a time. Save that for later. She crossed into the part of the city that held the noble houses but didn't spare them any of her attention. Her eyes were on the palace and on the people who might be a threat. She'd never be one of the Nine and had no family line to offer. Only herself, and her loyalty, which was owned by the Empress she served.

The guards at the outer circle of the royal grounds permitted her to pass without challenge, as did those closer in. Clearly, word of her impending arrival had spread. Thus, she wasn't surprised to see Gwyn waiting for her at the entrance. The Empress's seneschal was in formal clothes, robes that reached the floor and hid her shoes in a black and scarlet wave pattern.

There must have been a formal reception earlier.

The woman offered her a warm smile. "Hello, Champion."

Usha grinned. "It's been too long since I've been called that."

Her guide gestured for her to join her and turned to walk down the long corridor toward the interior of the palace. "Perhaps we are nearing the time when you will return to the city?"

She shrugged. "That, as always, is up to our ruler. How is she doing?"

"Perfectly, as ever." Something in the woman's tone caught her ear, and she stopped walking and touched her arm. Gwyn halted as well.

Usha looked around to be sure no one was present to overhear and asked, "Really?"

The seneschal nodded. "There are challenges, as there always are. The houses are squabbling."

She smiled. "To the Empress's distinct pleasure, no doubt."

The older woman laughed and started to walk again. "But of course. Anything that pulls problems away from her strengthens us all. Which, as I understand it, is why you're still living on the surface."

"Indeed. We are about to take a pivotal step in securing the city. That's the main reason I'm here."

"Do tell." Her voice was neutral but Usha heard the demand behind it. Shenni had told her more than once to trust Gwyn completely and she'd had no reason yet to doubt that command.

"I hope the Empress will provide us with Enforcers to strike a fatal blow at the heart of our enemy."

"Caliste Leblanc?"

"No, the girl is a tangential issue at the moment." She laughed. "I refer to the gang that opposes our expansion."

"Ahh. Well. You may find that our ruler does not agree with your assessment of Matriarch Leblanc."

She frowned as they turned the corner that led to the Empress's secluded work area away from the throne room and the other public areas of the palace. Once the guards who protected the section were out of earshot, she asked, "Why is that?"

Gwyn shrugged. "She is making herself known in New Atlantis. Firstly, she declared against the Malniets. Since then, she has fraternized with the Jehenel patriarch.

Finally, she soundly defeated an attack from Cormier. The girl appears to be as troublesome as her parents were."

Usha shook her head. "I handled that situation. If needed, I'll handle this one as well."

They reached the door and the seneschal opened it for her. "The Empress will be with you in a moment."

She stepped inside the office and the other woman closed the door behind her. While she could never conclusively identify how the seneschal knew what Shenni wanted, she assumed it was probably mind-to-mind contact of some kind.

Or other magic. Our ruler has access to all our records so who knows what she's discovered? Most of her believed that if secrets were found, they would be shared with her in order to increase her effectiveness. One smaller part doubted, though, and that portion of her consciousness grew more vocal with each passing day.

Her musings were interrupted by the arrival of the Empress. Shenni wore light robes in a rich shade of blue that varied like shadows in the deep ocean and she had eschewed makeup. Her ropy locks were piled atop her head and bound in cords with shells adorning them. She looked less calm than usual and less in command of herself. As she lowered herself into her chair, she pointed to the decanter on her desk and Usha poured two glasses. Her ruler drank and she did the same.

Shenni sighed. "Sword training." She shook her head. "This job is too sedentary and the captain of my guard seems to relish the opportunity to strike me. Damnable woman."

The gang leader laughed. "Now that sounds like a great

way to spend your day, Empress. Far more useful than sitting on the throne and dealing with matters of state."

The woman grinned. "I couldn't agree more. I realized I needed the exhaustion that a good daily workout would supply. Plus, although regaining my skills will take time, it has been a pleasure to feel the weight of a blade in my hand, even a practice one."

"Perhaps we should have a bout sometime?"

"Against a champion of New Atlantis?" The Empress laughed. "Hardly. I'm not in your league at the moment. I probably never was." She wasn't wrong. Where Usha's skills tended toward the martial end of the spectrum, Shenni's occupied the other side, the subtle knife rather than the drawn sword. "Anyway, what can I do for you today, Usha?"

"My Empress, I have come with good news. We are about to deliver two blows to decimate our rival gang in New Orleans. Once we have done so, the city will be yours for the taking as I promised."

The ruler frowned. "Indeed? Is that the most pressing issue at the moment?"

Usha stilled her features to avoid displaying the surprise that rippled through her. "I believe so—unless there has been a change of priority that I am unaware of?"

"What of Caliste Leblanc?" she asked and abruptly changed the subject.

"She has won another battle and has requested a meeting with us to discuss ending the ritual."

Empress Shenni leaned forward and tipped more rum into her glass. "Has she now? That is interesting. Very interesting. What are your intentions?"

Usha shrugged. "I had planned to speak to her, nothing more. I assumed you wished for us to keep her busy so that has been our objective. Well, and killing her, of course, within the rules—which has, admittedly, proven problematic."

Her ruler sighed and leaned back to stare at the ceiling. "I feel we are on the cusp of a moment of change but I can't identify what will happen. It's vexing. The girl is a part of it, without question. But so is House Malniet and possibly Jehenel."

The gang leader ventured a smile. "I have heard that the patriarch of that house has been seen at the palace now and then, Empress."

Shenni chuckled as she straightened again. "Rumors are useful, sometimes. He is connected to both Matriarch Leblanc and I, which is sure to confuse those who might consider action." She shook her head. "But something more is going on. I can't determine what it is but I know it's there. My spymaster feels the same."

"What would you have me do, Empress? I am, as ever, your devoted servant."

"That is the question, isn't it? Unfortunately, I don't yet have an answer. But when I do, you should be prepared to act without delay."

Usha nodded. "Of course." Inwardly, her concern that she'd done something to offend her ruler reached a higher level.

"So, what do you need for your grand effort against your rivals?" Shenni asked. Her tone was neither fully dismissive nor sarcastic, but she heard hints of both in her ruler's words.

"The usual, Empress. People—fighters, specifically. The first part of our plan will be easily accomplished with those I already have. But when we make our final strike, I would like to ensure that we have overwhelming force at our disposal."

The slow shake of Shenni's head was a spike of ice in her stomach. "No, I don't believe I can do that at this pivotal moment. My people are needed here to defend against whatever situation may be about to break. I'm afraid you'll need to handle this one on your own, Usha. That shouldn't be hard for the Champion of New Atlantis." When Gwyn had used the title, it had sounded like a compliment. Now, it made her feel small.

"Yes, Empress," she muttered.

Seemingly oblivious to the reaction she'd inspired, the woman waved her hand. "Go and return with word of your success." She had reclined to stare at the ceiling again and stayed in that position as Usha backed out of the room. Once the door had closed, she released the breath she'd held to keep herself from speaking.

"Champion, are you well?" Gwyn asked.

"Don't call me that." She turned and walked toward the exit.

Fine. If I have to bring the whole damn gang down with my own two hands, that's what I'll do.

217

Danna drummed her fingers on the table while she waited for the others to arrive. The lightweight suit she'd selected for the meeting was warmer than she'd prefer but she resisted the urge to pull at the collar of her shirt. It had been her decision to arrive at Cafe du Monde first to check the surroundings, and several members of her gang held position around the site. Across the street, Caliste Leblanc's friend did his magic routine. She was still upset that the gang member tasked with hurting him had managed to kill someone else. Neither the death nor the mistarget had been in her plans. The trap had almost caught the girl though.

And that was the key where she was concerned. *Almost, almost, and almost again. But we change and adapt.*

Today, she thought they'd get things going on the right track. When she'd shared the information about the blade that her alleged informant had provided with Usha, the other woman had been almost gleeful at the opportunity to ensnare the matriarch into the first move against the

Zatoras. Now, it was merely a matter of selling the idea to Caliste.

She wore an earbud with a channel to her sentries and was far from shocked when one reported that the Draksa had been located atop the Cathedral. That had been expected, and it was better for everyone if all the players were out in the open. The girl appeared from around the corner in her customary jean shorts, boots, and t-shirt. Danna grinned at the sight of the last item, as she was also a fan of The Pretty Reckless and eagerly awaited their new album.

That's something we have in common. We might as well become friends. She snorted and muttered a command into the wire that connected the earbud to her phone.

Caliste took the seat across from her and she offered her a grin. "Welcome, Matriarch. There's no need to dress up for us or anything."

The girl nodded. "Good. I'm glad to hear it. Where's your boss?"

"On her way. Where's your dragon?"

She chuckled. "Nearby, and I'm sure you already had the answer to that question, exactly like I know the last member of our party is walking down the street right now." She twisted and pulled her red hair back to reveal the earpiece she wore.

Danna laughed and lifted her iced coffee to her lips. Locals would consider it sacrilege but she simply couldn't do hot drinks in the sun. *Not now and not ever.* Usha rounded the corner in a multicolored dress that showed a fair amount of skin but nonetheless conveyed an air of power and mastery. Her boss sat in the chair beside her and kept the table as a separator between opposing sides.

Cali nodded. "Usha."

"Matriarch Leblanc."

The girl rolled her eyes. "Must we?"

The Atlantean leader chuckled. "No, I suppose we mustn't. Cali."

"So, how about we let this whole ritual combat process slide, hmm?"

Usha shook her head. "I can't do it. But I have a counteroffer that might interest you in place of that request."

Caliste sighed and looked tired for an instant before she assumed a blank expression. "And what would that be?"

"We know where another fragment of your house sword is," Danna replied. "And we have important information. It'll soon disappear."

She straightened in her chair. "Are you threatening to make it disappear?"

Usha lifted a hand with the palm out. "No, nothing of the sort. In this, we have a common enemy. Rion Grisham has the sword at his mansion."

The girl frowned and folded her arms. "Tell me something I don't know."

"We will, but it counts as your boon," the second in command answered. "Otherwise, ask something else and we'll certainly consider the request." She gave an appropriately condescending grin, merely to play with her.

Leblanc growled with undisguised irritation. "This is so stupid. Fine. Tell me, and we'll call the last battle even."

Usha smiled and in the expression, Danna saw the pleasure she took in the pieces of her plan falling together so neatly. "We have a source—one who saved my life the other night from a Zatora attack. Grisham plans to go underground and leave the mansion for more secure territory. You're about to lose your chance to get the blade."

She couldn't hide the alarm in her eyes, although she did a decent job of keeping her feelings out of her expression. "When?"

"Tomorrow. If you don't take it tonight, you probably never will."

She and Fyre sprinted from the tavern basement into the common room and startled Janice, who was finishing with the Tuesday lunch crowd. The girl almost dropped her tray but managed to catch it, and Cali was pretty sure she saw Zeb's fingers move.

I bet he can do telekinesis too, dammit.

Cali climbed on the stool, and he delivered a cider to her and leaned on the bar. "What's going on?"

After a sip, she shook her head. "Wait for Tanyith. He'll be here soon and I'll only have to tell the story once."

He clapped briskly. "Oh, this is a good one, then. I can't wait." His voice was such that she couldn't identify if it was kidding or mocking, which was something she always appreciated in him. Both she and the Draksa enjoyed a meal of stew until finally, her partner entered through the main door.

She spun in the chair. "What took you so long?"

He rolled his eyes. "I was across town and sleeping when you texted. I had to shower to wake up."

"Slacker."

He sat beside her. "Okay, what's so urgent?"

"Grisham is moving out of the mansion tonight and going underground. I guess he might leave someone else in charge of the day to day?" She shrugged. "I'm not sure what it means for the gang as a whole, but it means a whole lot for my ability to get the shard I need."

Tanyith frowned. "And how do you know this?"

She sighed. "From the Atlanteans. We had our sit-down." He looked like he intended to chide her and she added, "Fyre was close. It was fine. But there's no reason not to believe them. Anything bad for him is good for them, and if we attack his house before he leaves, it would probably count as bad in his book."

Zeb leaned closer with a concerned frown. "Okay, this might only be random coincidence, but when the Zatoras targeted Vizidus, someone said it was a farewell from Grisham. Maybe this is what they meant."

Tanyith folded his arms. "This is as suspicious as hell, people. You do see that, right? The Atlanteans already know you're looking for pieces of weapons and they used that against you before. Why do you think this is any different?"

Cali shook her head. "I don't. There's undoubtedly a layer of something going on that's still hidden. But it doesn't change anything. We need to retrieve the shard eventually. I planned to do it later since we knew its location, but I don't see any particular reason to wait. We'll simply do it first."

"And tick off the entire Zatora organization when we attack their mansion again."

She resisted the urge to slam her fists on the bar and finished her cider instead while she considered her reply. "Look. I get it. I totally get it. But even if it is a trap, if there's any truth to it, I have to recover the shard before it vanishes. Otherwise, Atreo will never be free."

Tanyith ran his hands through his hair like he wanted to pull it out of his scalp. "We could find the piece again."

"Can you guarantee that? A life literally depends upon it."

"No. Of course not." He sighed. "But this is a bad, bad idea, Cali."

"I know. But will you do it with me?"

He gave a hopeless sounding laugh. "Yeah. Definitely."

Zeb seemed about to offer but she shook her head. "No, it'll only be the three of us. We're already on their...uh, bad list. You have some deniability left. And if we are arrested or something, we'll need you to bail us out."

And if I don't make it, I'll need you to break the news to Emalia.

He nodded slowly. "Okay. But you have to talk the whole plan through in front of me and then, we'll see how to improve it. And if you get in trouble, portal here where I can assist you."

"Agreed."

The dwarf shook his head. "I'll also put the council on alert. The boy's right—this sounds like a trap and it could easily be part of something bigger." He departed to the corner of the bar and seemed to talk to the air like he had done before.

Tanyith gestured at him with his chin and asked, "What is with that?"

She shook her head. "Obviously not telepathy. Maybe it's like verbal text messages among old magicals? I don't know but I've seen him do it before when the council was involved."

He chuckled. "I doubt he'd appreciate being called old."

"I call 'em as I see 'em. He makes you look almost young, which is really saying something." She recalled the early insults Barton had thrown at him about dating someone as young as Cali. "But I still won't go out with you."

He grinned. "That's good. Kendra would probably shoot you."

Cali brightened. "Hey, we have the stun guns from Diana. Maybe I could try one on her."

"Behave. But taking them along tonight is a great idea."

She nodded and stood on the footrest of her chair to peer over the bar. "What do you think, buddy? It's almost certainly a trap, but should we do it anyway?"

Fyre raised his head to look her in the eye, nodded deliberately, and put it down and closed his eyes. She sat with a laugh. "See, he's already preparing."

Tanyith chuckled. "Too bad we all can't sleep that much, right?"

"We'll sleep once New Orleans is no longer under the thumbs of the Atlanteans, the Zatoras, or whoever else wants to mess with our town."

"Don't forget New Atlantis."

"Right. There, too. But maybe a nap between." Her spirits soared and confidence flowed through her.

All right, Atreo, brother mine. We'll take another step in the right direction tonight.

CHAPTER TWENTY-SEVEN

The atmosphere in the bunker was filled with energy. Cali pulled her uniform on faster than usual and took the effort to pack her other concerns away equally quickly. She hadn't been this full of hope for some time, and while she thought a smart person would probably slow and investigate the feeling a little, she didn't have any interest in being that individual at the moment.

She snatched one of Invel's glass globes and tossed it high in an arc toward Tanyith. "Think quick."

He flinched but caught the sphere with telekinesis and brought it to his hand. "Thanks."

"That wasn't cool."

"It's not my fault you suck at basic magic." He laughed.

Fyre snorted from where he paced along the wall that held the pictures and the string. She twisted to look at him. "Shut it, you." A wave of mirth washed over her, and she grinned. "Maybe you should take another nap. You've only had seven today."

The Draksa breathed frost at her feet, which drew

laughter from both her and Tanyith. She stood, fully outfitted and with potions on both legs, two crystal globes in a pouch at her waist, and her necklaces with the Leblanc symbol and the magic charms showing. Her final action was to retrieve the holster that had come with the stun gun and secure it to her belt at her right hand. The extra cartridge went into a jacket pocket.

Her partner looked at her and shook his head. "You look more violent by the day."

She pulled her hair back and bound it with a tie, then added two more to keep her unruly curls in place. "I'm not bad. I'm only drawn that way."

He chuckled. "Now you're doing movie quotes too?"

"The troll rubbed off on me." She grinned. "What can I say?"

"Yeah, that one is something. They all are."

Cali nodded and checked her watch again. They'd decided to strike around eleven on the assumption the household might go to bed early if they were planning a move. Tanyith and a veiled Fyre had done reconnaissance earlier but had discovered nothing conclusive. Ultimately, the Zatora plans didn't matter. They'd go in and hope for the best.

They were in complete agreement on one thing, though. If the object they sought was there, it would be in Grisham's room of treasures. She feared he'd lock it away in a safe but her partner convinced her he'd want the shard where he could see it since he considered it a collector's item. If he was wrong and the Zatora leader had secured the sword piece, she planned to put a portal under whatever safe protected it and let it drop into the basement of the tavern where they could deal with the lock at leisure.

And maybe ask Diana and her techs for help.

Tanyith slipped his Sai into place with a twirl. She pointed her chin at them. "How did you wind up with those?"

He shrugged. "I thought I was cool, I guess. We all chose something that would make us stand out. Others had fancy guns or big knives. One of them even had a miniature crossbow. It was a stupid game, especially since we broke the law and did so with memorable weaponry." He laughed and shook his head. "Man, we were dumb."

"Don't sell yourself short. You're still dumb."

The man stuck his tongue out at her before finishing. "Anyway, I saw a kung fu film that used these and kind of fell in love with how they looked. Then I decided it would be great to actually know how to use them. And here we are." He gestured at her wrist. "I'd trade them for magic weapons in an instant, though."

She nodded. "They are cool, especially now that I can catch magic and cast my own with the sticks." She paused to let him think she wouldn't continue, then broke into a grin. "And if we find any you can use among my parents' things that aren't heirlooms, you've got dibs."

He laughed. "Am I that obvious?"

"I've noticed your lustful looks at my Escrima sticks, yes. It's shameful." Fyre snorted and she waved a hand in his direction. "See, he thinks so too."

Tanyith shook his head as he stood and stretched. "Man, it's good not to have the damn Malniets' compulsion on me anymore." He practiced drawing the stun pistol and frowned. "That feels really weird."

Cali tried hers and had to agree. "Maybe we should carry them rather than trying to draw them when we see an enemy. And probably not rely on being able to yank them out at need."

"Agreed."

She checked her watch. *Ten-thirty. To hell with it.* She looked up. "How about we go do this thing?"

Her companions were on their feet beside her before she finished the sentence, clearly as eager as she was to get the night's activities underway.

As she stepped from the portal, she surveyed the grounds surrounding the Zatora Mansion, which were the same as they had been the last time she'd been there. It seemed like a lifetime before, given how much had happened since then. But there, at least on the exterior, nothing had changed.

A closer look at the house ahead revealed how wrong she was. "Are those metal sheets?"

Tanyith nodded. "Yeah. I didn't mention them because they don't change anything materially, given that we assumed the windows would be trapped anyway. But they've become very serious about physical security."

"Covering all the windows seems a little extreme."

He shrugged. "Paranoia, I guess."

She frowned. "This makes it less likely that he's about to leave to go somewhere safer, you know?"

"I thought about that. But like you said earlier, it doesn't matter. We'd have to do this eventually so it might as well be tonight."

With a sigh, she looked at Fyre, who gazed out into the distance. "How about it, buddy? Do you still think this is a good idea?"

"Yep. We've fooled around with all these idiots too long. We have to knock them down somewhere and this is as fine a place as any." He walked forward slowly and she and Tanyith fell into step with him.

"Okay. So we stick to the plan. Break the door in and fight our way from there. Speed will be key. The only reason we stop is if one of us is stuck. Otherwise, it's in, up, and directly to the treasure room. Once we have what we need, we can portal out."

Tanyith nodded. "It's a good plan—as little contact as possible, as little damage as possible, and in and out quickly."

Fyre didn't reply and only stared ahead and started to walk a little faster. Cali asked, "Do you see any wards outside, Tay?"

He paused, then replied, "Nope. My guess is they have cameras and other security though, so let's do this." The air rippled with magic as he cast a veil over them both, and Fyre's form shimmered as he activated his illusion.

"Okay. Remember—fast, safe, and get it done and don't get distracted."

Inside the mansion, Ozahl sat at a table with Rion

Grisham, Jack Strang, and Colin Todd. He'd contrived excuses to delay the meeting and claimed to be gathering information about their enemies. It was vital that Todd, at least, be present when their patsy made her move. Danna had confirmed that she and Usha had planted the threat of losing the sword if she didn't act immediately, so the fun would definitely happen sometime that night. He'd also ensured that Lila and Dalton were nowhere around since there was no way to predict what kind of chaos might ensue.

Grisham growled his annoyance yet again. "How could we have failed to kill her? Let's go over it one more time."

The mage shrugged. "I wasn't there. I was at a different ambush site. But from what I hear, it was bad luck. They had a car with extra armor and reacted more aggressively than our people expected them to. For all we know, all the cars the wench uses are equally reinforced. In any case, from all the reports I've gathered, the first shot missed and from there, magic won the day."

He'd spent much of the previous two days convincing the others that it wasn't a big deal, that the failure was simply random happenstance and bad luck, and that they should wait a week or so before they tried again so the enemy's vigilance would settle. He believed his involvement in foiling the ambush was still secret, although Todd constantly stared at him at odd moments as if he had something he wanted to say but couldn't quite bring himself to do it.

Tonight, the accountant-like lieutenant wore a sharp black suit but no tie. His black shoes shone. *Perfect funeral attire.* He, Strang, and even Grisham were in business casual, which was a step up for him, sartorially speaking, and a step down for them.

Strang's low voice observed, "Next time, you should be there."

Ozahl chuckled. "Yes, well, I agree, my friend. If we fight magicals, I should be there. And if I can't be, we shouldn't do it." He turned to Grisham and offered the man a syrupy smile. "But I'm sure there were reasons I'm not privy to why we did it the way we did."

The Zatora leader stared hard at him and he feared he'd pushed him too far. A surprisingly large part of him hoped he had. *Come on, you bastard. If you want to do it, let's do it. We'll decide how to pick up the pieces of our plan after and make them fit right.* He summoned his magic, ready to blast his way through the other three men.

The boss shook his head. "No. I got ahead of myself and that won't happen again. But let there be no mistake. That witch will die. And tonight, we'll think of a way to make it happen."

He seemed about to say something else but a crash from the area of the entrance door followed immediately by shouting cut him off. Ozahl grinned.

Welcome to the party, Matriarch Leblanc. Your timing is perfect.

CHAPTER TWENTY-EIGHT

Tanyith blasted the doors from their hinges and hurled them into the main area and trapped two guards beneath them. Cali surged through and jumped on the left door, while Fyre matched her on the other one. Their landings elicited groans from below. Motion to her left caught her attention and she spun and pulled the trigger on the stun gun. The blast missed her target by several feet and shattered the front of an ornate china cabinet.

"Damn it...stupid gun." She thrust the stick in her left hand out and a burst of force lifted the guard she'd missed with the pistol and flung him into the wall. The sound of crackling from behind her signaled Fyre icing the connection between rooms on that side. Tanyith raced past her, headed to the next room and the stairs that lay in the one beyond it. His stun gun discharged several times and when she crossed the threshold, the bodies of his targets came into view.

"Good shooting, Tex," she yelled,

He laughed, then dropped with a yelp. She threw herself down as three guards appeared on the balcony above with rifles. Their first shots missed and Cali scrambled to use the staircase banister as cover. Her partner used his telekinesis to pull at one of the weapons, and the strap it was attached to yanked its owner over the railing. He fell with a loud cry that ended abruptly when he landed. The more mentally agile of the two remaining enemies yelled, "Magic," and both simultaneously released the magazines from the bottom of their weapons.

"Oh, hell," Cali muttered and forced magic into her muscles. She pounded up the stairs and pitted her speed against their ability to insert new magazines that could only be filled with anti-magic bullets. The top step came earlier than expected, while her body moved faster than it ever had before. The closest one turned as he pushed up on the long, curved ammunition holder, and she zapped him with the stun gun. He fell as if in slow motion.

Fyre's scream exploded in her head. "Down!" She obeyed without question and a wash of frost flew above her to freeze the other guard an instant before he could pull the trigger.

There wasn't time to process the fact that the Draksa had spoken into her mind. She felt triumph from him and no words were sufficient to capture her emotions at the moment. Instead, she called, "Forward," and raced to the side of the mansion that held Grisham's bedroom and treasure closet.

Ozahl had positioned himself between the other two men and Colin Todd at the first sound of trouble.

Grisham snapped, "Go see what's going on."

Immediately, he countered with, "Strang, stay here and protect the boss. We'll check it out." Always the good underling, Todd didn't complain and hurried to the door.

All right, we need to get close to them before I can pull it off. Of course, if he dies in the crossfire, that would be fine, too.

"Get behind me," he muttered to keep up appearances and summoned a force shield on his left hand. He kept his right free for use in offensive spells. Once he saw what kind the girl used, he'd know what to choose to implement his plan. His companion obeyed and he led the way out through the kitchen into the main hallway from which the staircase led upward. The moaning and twitching body of a guard who had apparently fallen from above sprawled in the middle, and he stepped carefully past him to look up. "All clear, let's go."

"How do you know where they're headed?" Todd asked and sounded suspicious,

Ozahl sighed, stopped, and turned at the person he was itching to kill. Part of his reply was an act, but the emotion behind it was real. "Are you an idiot? Clearly, that man"— he pointed at the fallen figure—"was recently up there." He raised a finger to the balcony. "Obviously, they went that way. I don't know what you people would do without me— probably get yourselves killed by the first magical you encountered."

He turned and stalked away. The sputtering behind him remained close so his primary goal was still viable. When they reached the top of the stairs, he pointed to one of the downed guards. "Take his gun. It looks like he has anti-magic loaded. That'll be useful." The other man did as he was told and held it carefully with the barrel pointed at the ceiling.

Todd asked, "Who is it?"

The mage shrugged. "My guess it's the Atlanteans. We targeted their leader so they're after ours. They must have assumed he'd be in bed. It's the last mistake they'll make." Gunfire and shouts issued from the rooms ahead, and he grinned. "It sounds like we're going the right way, doesn't it?"

The layout had changed since the previous time they'd been there. What had been Grisham's bedroom was now a study and three guards played cards inside, apparently taking advantage of their boss's absence. Cali managed to stun one, but the other two opened fire. She released her left stick and flung a force shield up to catch the bullets but had to retreat as they separated to create more advantageous firing lines.

Tanith pushed past her and shot one with his stun gun, and the man fell. She shoved her pistol into its holster and blasted the remaining guard with lightning. Her control wasn't perfect but it was enough to make him jitter and dance before he collapsed senseless to the floor. She moved forward and mentally told Fyre, "Ice 'em."

"Will do," he replied in the same way and she grinned

again at the new level of connection they'd found. The next chamber was huge, as Grisham had knocked out the wall that used to be there to create a bedroom that also served as a treasure room. Art and items covered the walls, and she could almost picture the Zatora leader in the space among his treasures, filled with self-admiration for his many accomplishments.

For a moment, she had the urge to search for him simply to punch him in the mouth for how he acted in her mind but shook it off. "Find the shard."

She and Tanyith spread out to look. After a couple of moments, Fyre entered as well and took a position near the door on the far side of the room in case any enemies came through it. She ransacked cabinets and searched through drawers but couldn't find anything that looked like what they'd come for. "Anything?" she called,

Tanyith sounded as frustrated as she felt. "Nothing, dammit. Where is it?"

A voice from the doorway replied, "Whatever you're looking for, you won't get it." They turned to a bookish man with a rifle aimed at Cali's head. "They're anti-magic bullets, and if I hear one sound, she's dead. Now, slowly, move together to the center of the room."

Ozahl froze behind Todd. He hadn't expected the guy to be so downright martial. He couldn't risk anything that might make him pull the trigger because Caliste was key to their current plan and a part of their New Atlantis strategy as well. A great deal depended on her survival, at least for a little longer. It was one of the reasons why Danna hadn't put all that much effort into preparing the opponents the girl faced in her ritual battles. While they had other options, they didn't have better ones than the young matriarch.

He stepped behind his alleged ally and whispered, "Grisham will want to talk to her so try not to kill her. Keep calm." The Zatora lieutenant ignored him and gestured with the rifle.

"Move it, now," the man in the doorway instructed. She obeyed and sent a mental message to Fyre to wait for the right moment. Tanyith stepped slowly toward her, both careful not to spook the person who aimed the gun at them. She partitioned her mind and sent part of it out searching. His defenses were laughable and in moments, she was inside his head.

"How about you drop that weapon?" she suggested. In his mind, she commanded his hands to do it and while the rifle didn't leave his grasp, his finger did come off the trigger. What happened next was completely unexpected. He careened into the room like he'd been pushed and the gun clattered away as he stumbled forward. She dodged instinctively, and a man she didn't recognize stepped into the doorway. He was sloppily dressed and entirely average looking.

Tanyith sounded shocked as he muttered, "Aiden."

The man grinned. "Hello again, Tanyith. I heard you were around. Long time." Then, without preamble, he raised his hands and dispatched twin bolts of lightning, both of them very well contained in wicked ropes that twined across the room.

CHAPTER TWENTY-NINE

F yre moved and Tanyith did too. She remained frozen and watched the lines of confined energy burn into the chest and head of the man who'd had the rifle and who had twisted as he'd stumbled into the room. She couldn't quite process what was going on.

Magic careened in the other direction as both Tanyith and Fyre attacked, but the man he'd called Aiden had already backed away with his shields raised. He laughed, then turned and ran. In the distance, she heard him yell, "Up here. They've killed Colin Todd."

She exchanged horrified looks with Tanyith, then pushed her questions and worries away. "Fyre, ice both entrances. No one gets in here. Keep them up until I say otherwise." He instantly moved to obey and she turned to Tanyith. "We can't afford to be subtle. Blast everything that might contain it. The magic shouldn't hurt the blade, right?"

He shrugged. "Who knows? It sounds logical, though." He began to use force bursts to demolish vases, statues, and furniture. She did the same on the opposite side of the room. After a couple of minutes, voices from beyond the ice were interspersed by the sound of bullet ricochets.

"I guess ice is ice," Cali said, "whether it's magical or not. That's handy. Take that, Zatoras." She used a line of force to shatter the mirror over a dresser and noticed a glint when it spun from the impact. Excitement thrummed and she tiptoed forward, barely breathing, and tried not to hope. But there it was—the silver shard of her family's sword, if their evidence was right, remained attached to its hiding place on the back of the rotating mirror. "I have it, Tay. Get us out of here." She snatched a blanket from the demolished bed and wrapped her prize, then ran through the portal her partner had created. Fyre was through next, and the man stepped across and dropped his magic.

They stood together in the basement of the Drunken Dragons Tavern and grinned stupidly at each other. She knelt and set the fabric down, then revealed the blade fragment for them to see. Tanyith nodded. "It looks exactly right. I think we got it." He sounded partly relieved and partly happy, but it was colored with anger. She looked at him.

"Who was that?"

He shook his head. "Let's talk about that later. We don't want to be here any longer in case they come looking. Stick to the plan."

Cali nodded and opened a portal to New Atlantis, and they stepped through to what was currently the safest place on the planet for her, the estate of House Leblanc.

She and Tanyith had taken showers and changed into the more comfortable clothes they each kept in the mansion. Fyre awaited them in the kitchen, as did Emalia. A portal to the tavern showed Zeb seated on a crate smoking, and he immediately strode through to join them. Her great aunt passed coffee all around, and Cali set the shard on the table and unwrapped it.

The dwarf nodded at it. "So this is the thing that will free your brother?"

"Part of it. There are still more pieces and I need information from House Malniet, but this is a definite step in the right direction."

Tanyith frowned and the older woman noticed. "What's the matter?" she asked him.

He sighed. "Someone died tonight. We didn't kill him but we'll be blamed for it."

Zeb growled with displeasure. "Who was it?"

Tanyith shook his head. "I'm not sure, but I think Aiden called him Colin."

Cali nodded. "I heard Todd. So, Colin Todd or Todd Colin."

"Either way, he's one of Grisham's right-hand people. I saw him a while back in a Zatora warehouse when I was looking for Aiden."

Emalia interrupted. "Who's this Aiden?"

He shrugged and laughed helplessly. "Ah, that's the question of the moment. Aiden Walsh is the person my ex-girlfriend asked me to find. He's an Atlantean gang member from the good old days. He's also, apparently, another of Grisham's closest people and the dude who killed our man with two first names."

The dwarf frowned. "Wait. He killed his ally?"

"That's what I saw."

Cali sighed. "Yeah. Same here."

Fyre, from under the table, added, "Yes."

She shook her head. "So, it was a trap but not the kind we thought."

Tanyith put his head in his hands. "It makes my brain hurt. Why the hell would he kill his own guy? And it can't be a coincidence that we were there when it happened."

"Not a chance. No, my guess is that he was aware we were coming and turned it to his advantage. Which begs the question of how he knew."

Zeb drummed his fingers on the table. "This guy...was he kind of unimpressive looking? Way more powerful than it seemed he should be?"

"Yeah, sounds like a good description," the man replied,

He nodded. "That's how Vizidus and his wife described their attacker. Who also mentioned something about Grisham leaving town."

"Holy hell," Cali interjected. "Are you saying what I think you're saying? This guy fed information to everyone? Played all sides against each other so he'd have the chance to kill the other dude?"

Emalia spoke and her tone carried the calm confidence of a teacher in a classroom. "The evidence fits but that doesn't mean it's the only possibility."

The girl laughed and looked at Tanyith. "We need to get her and Nylotte into a room and see who comes out with their brain broken." He grinned and her great aunt stared at her like she'd lost her mind. "Ignore me. It doesn't matter. The important part is we have another piece of the puzzle. We're one step closer to our goal."

Zeb nodded in agreement. "That we are. So, what's next?"

She yawned. "I won't be able to drop this off with Alessand until tomorrow, so I guess it's sleep for me. You're all welcome to stay. Jenkins can get you situated." She stood and stretched. "The portal service to the surface will be tomorrow morning. We need to find out what game Tanyith's old friend is playing."

After Cali and Fyre left, Tanyith looked across the table at Zeb. The dwarf's expression was hard. "What trouble isn't she seeing?" he asked bluntly

"From what I hear, Aiden Walsh is a certified badass with very little in the way of a conscience. On my rating scale, he's scarier by far than the Zatoras, the Atlanteans we've fought, and probably whoever Cali's facing here." He shook his head. "This is not a good development."

He nodded. "You think Walsh wanted her there so he could pin the killing on her."

"I do."

"To go to the police?"

Tanyith shook his head. "I can't see that. No, he's up to something else."

Zeb shrugged. "Well, all we can do is keep our eyes open and be ready to roll with the punches. And all you can do is tell me what the hell is in that bag you're fondling."

He laughed and removed the velvet sack he'd taken from Grisham's bedroom from under the table. When he'd first looked inside, he'd hardly believed it, and as the gems tumbled out, he continued to have problems accepting it as reality. "I call it scumbag tax and a bonus for finally finding damned Aiden Walsh." Diamonds glittered on the table. He flicked one to his companion. "Start me a tab, bartender."

The dwarf laughed and held it to the light. "This will keep you in stew and cider for quite some time, my friend."

He separated half the gems and returned them to the bag, then stowed it in a pocket. The remainder, he pushed to Zeb. "For Cali. She's more than earned it." He turned and walked up the stairs to his room, keenly aware of the dwarf's eyes drilling into his back.

I know. No amount of money will make up for me bringing my past enemies into her present. But I'll be at her side to resolve it out no matter what, which is all I can do.

CHAPTER THIRTY

O n the surface, the Zatora Mansion was in disarray. Grisham was furious, as out of control as Ozahl had ever seen him. Every gang member had been called to the site and they worked to gather everything essential and shove it into numerous cars that had been assembled outside the entrance.

He'd concocted the story that they'd leave the building and now, it had come true. For some reason, that made him chuckle inwardly. Jack Strang stormed around angrily and he had the sense the huge man and Colin Todd might have been friends. He hadn't seen that coming at all. In fact, more ambient sadness about the man's death permeated the house than he'd expected.

A more perplexing issue was that he wasn't sure how much of Grisham's anger sprang from the demise of his lieutenant, which made it difficult to determine the right time to suggest a big funeral. He'd pretended respect for the dead, put a mournful expression on his face, and used his magic to help the guards wrap his body in a white sheet and transport it to one of the vans. They had a funeral home connection, apparently.

The thing he found most frustrating was that the Zatora leader felt the need for security in numbers. He never left a room without Strang and at least two guards, and they managed to keep him from getting the man alone to plant the idea. Which meant he'd need to stay close too.

Ozahl pulled his phone out and summoned Lila and Dalton now that the dangerous action was over. They texted immediately and gave an eta that suggested they'd stayed nearby to be close at hand. Since he'd have to leave sometimes in order to keep the other balls he had in the air in motion, they could stay near the big man for him when necessary. He'd have to let them in on the next part of his plan in case the need arose to block a suggestion that wasn't a big funeral.

Despite his frustration, he shrugged. It had worked out so far so there was no reason to think it wouldn't continue to do so. He wanted to call Danna and let her know what had transpired, but he would do so only in an emergency unless he was in private, and privacy wasn't an option right now.

A crash issued from the direction in which Grisham and Strang had headed and a loud curse that might have been from either of them followed. With a sigh, Ozahl put on a concerned frown and strode toward the noise while he tried his best to look sincere.

Across town, in the main room of the Shark Nightclub, the band was rocking hard, the crowd was rowdy, and Usha and Danna tossed drinks back in celebration. Word had come from the people they had watching that the Zatora mansion was in chaos, which they both took to mean the ploy with Caliste Leblanc had worked.

"When will you know?" the Atlantean leader asked.

The other woman shook her head. "There's no way to be sure. My source knows his safety is the most important thing, so I imagine he'll lie low for a while." *Which is unfortunate, because I feel like celebrating.* "Doubtless he'll need a fix before too long, which should bring him out from cover." *Heh. Well, we are kind of addicted to each other.* The endgame seemed close for the first time in forever. While a fair number of steps still remained before they'd take their places among the Nine, the foundation was finally being set in place.

Her boss broke her mental wanderings with the snap of her fingers in front of her eyes. They both laughed. "Who are you thinking about?" Usha asked.

She grinned. "Who says it's a who?"

"I've known you for a long time. It's definitely a who. So, out with it. Is there a particular someone?"

A shock raced through her as she realized she'd stumbled into a pivotal moment with no clue it was coming. One of the big questions all along had been how to bring Usha in and how to use the gang for their own ends without losing connection to the woman she loved more than anyone save Ozahl. And there it was—a way to begin. She smiled. "Actually, there is."

She nodded sagely. "How long?"

Forever. "A few dates. But it's going well. I think it might be real."

Usha hugged her quickly. "Good for you. But if he or she tries to take you away from me, I'll have to kill them. Just so we're clear."

Danna laughed. "I'll make sure he knows. I don't imagine it'll scare him off, though."

The other woman ordered another round of drinks from the bar and when they came, lifted her glass in a toast. "To your happiness. May you get everything out of life that you want."

She clinked and drank. *And may you want everything we'll offer you.*

Miles away and far, far down, Patriarch Styrris Malniet stepped into Shenni's private office with a smile. He was very well dressed in a charcoal suit with a pale green shirt that buttoned to the neck and a pendant in place of a tie. It had a black face with a silver hook upon it, and the sharp lines and wicked barbs made the symbol seem inherently violent.

The severe features of the leader of House Malniet conveyed the same impression. His short dark hair was perfectly combed, his angular cheekbones made his face seem long and disapproving, and his thin body seemed nonetheless ready to strike like a whip. He radiated more calm menace than anyone she'd ever met.

But he was only one of the Nine, and she was the Empress of New Atlantis. Her dress was designed to impress. It clung to her figure in scarlet with black accents and left much of her chest, her arms, and most of her legs bare. She rarely wore high heels but today, for him, she had selected the pair she liked best. Also as a boon for him, she sat in one of the side chairs rather than putting the desk between them. Only a small table would separate them once he joined her.

It was a breach of etiquette that he did not kneel but only bowed and kissed her hand before he sat. That had been the tradition in the first Atlantis and if pressed, he would doubtless claim to simply follow the oldest rules of their culture. It wasn't a reason for action on her part but it was worth notice.

After he had taken his seat, Gwyn entered with drinks on a tray—heavily spiced dark rum with a single ice cube for them both. The tumblers were the finest crystal, discovered in one of the many shipwrecks that surrounded the city. The rules always permitted her first choice from salvages, and while she usually took only a personal low-value item, these had spoken to her.

Her visitor sipped and finally broke the silence. "Empress. Thank you for the invitation."

She chuckled. "Oh, so formal, Styrris. I appreciate you coming."

The edge of his thin mouth quirked. "As if I had a choice."

Shenni shrugged. "It is one of the privileges of rank, as you well know, Patriarch."

He nodded. "So, I presume this is not purely a social visit?"

"You presume correctly. Tell me, what are your plans where Leblanc is concerned?"

Styrris shook his head slightly. "Upstarts. They will be destroyed—properly this time."

She took another sip and looked at him from under a lowered brow. "From what I hear, accomplishing that has proven to be a challenge. And all know that yours is not the most...populous house." His alleged fertility issues were a source of instant irritation for him as she well knew, and she enjoyed darting across that line whenever she interacted with the man. *Privileges of rank indeed.*

The man shrugged. "We have extended relatives to draw upon. They will be adequate." The way he said it was an invitation.

One she accepted. "It so happens that I think I can help you with that situation."

"In return for what, Empress?"

Shenni smiled. "Your assistance in a game I've undertaken. I have other options but there's a certain poetic justice to finishing House Leblanc now that the last scion of that house has appeared."

He chuckled. "Shattering their heirloom sword wasn't enough for you?"

She finished her drink. "It was but a start, my friend. I've thought lately that nine is too many. Fewer houses equal more power. Are you interested?"

Finally, a true smile spread across his face. "I must admit that I am."

"Excellent," she said and sent a mental message to

Gwyn. "Let's talk over dinner about which houses should remain and which should suffer an unexpected demise."

The End

The story doesn't end here. Continue fighting the chaos in *Enchanted Twist*!

If you enjoyed this book, you may also enjoy the first series from T.R. Cameron, also set in the Oriceran Universe. The Federal Agents of Magic series begins with Magic Ops and it's available now at Amazon and through Kindle Unlimited.

FBI Agent Diana Sheen is an agent with a secret...

...She carries a badge and a troll, along with a little magic.

But her Most Wanted List is going to take a little extra effort.

She'll have to embrace her powers and up her game to take down new threats,

Not to mention deal with the troll that's adopted her.

All signs point to a serious threat lurking just beyond sight, pulling the strings to put the forces of good in harm's way.

Magic or mundane, you break the law, and Diana's gonna find you, tag you and bring you in. Watch out magical baddies, this agent can level the playing field.

It's all in a day's work for the newest Federal Agent of Magic.

Available now at Amazon and through Kindle Unlimited

Thank you for reading the sixth book in the Scions of Magic series! I had a ton of fun writing this one, although I was sad not to manage to include any giant creatures for Cali to fight. Maybe next book.

We're nearing the end of this part of Cali's tale. The series is planned to end with book eight (which means things are going to move fast for Cali and company from here on out!), and then I'll be on to something else new and exciting with Martha and Michael. I hope you'll come along for whatever adventure is next!

I'm finding myself in a strange place this spring. I'm not sure if it's all the ambient stress of political season or what, but I'm seeking comfort in gaming, reading, and other media more often than usual. I'll be sharing some stuff on Facebook about that, including some of the quick-hit brain candy I've been enjoying most.

My wife and I are about to finish watching Peaky Blinders on Netflix. Aside from the fact that Cillian Murphy has to be the handsomest man on the planet, the show is really well written and spectacularly acted. There are a few slow points, and the total style shift at the start of season five is kind of shifting without a clutch, but I totally recommend it if you're into gangster films, underworld power politics, and such. Which, let's be fair, if you like my books you probably are.

We have too many video game systems. I've been an Xbox guy for a long time, so we have an Xbox One. My kid scammed me into getting a Nintendo Switch to be able to play with a friend, and then double-scammed me for a gaming computer to play Minecraft with mods. (And allegedly to start a YouTube gaming channel. Still waiting on that one to materialize) Somewhere in the middle, my wife decided she had to play Death Stranding, because she's obsessed with Mads Mikkelsen, so we have that, too.

Long story short (too late), the Bioshock collection was the PS Plus freebie this month, so I dove back in for a trip to Rapture. Bioshock 1 and 2 were as amazing as I remembered. Bioshock Infinite, I'm trying to ignore the huge story problems to enjoy the gameplay, but only with moderate success. Still, story-wise, it's a good time to be alive with all the options we have!

Altered Carbon season two is the next thing on my list. I'll be really interested to see how they manage the re-sleeving of Kovacs. Will the new actor imitate the old? How will a different body influence the character? Should be really wild.

Daily family game time has become surprisingly cutthroat. I blame the game Exploding Kittens, because it encourages you to gang up on other players. Turns out my kid has a vicious streak as a game player. Sniff. I'm so proud.

Until next time, Joys upon joys to you and yours – so may it be.

PS: If you'd like to chat with me, here's the place. I check in daily or more: https://www.facebook.com/AuthorTRCameron. For more info on my books, and to join my reader's group, please visit www.trcameron.com.

AUTHOR NOTES - MARTHA CARR

MARCH 20, 2020

Charley Case is the giant redheaded, bearded quiet rebel in our midst who can be very Zen when you least expect it. He's going to go his own way and will gladly invite along anyone who has a similar yen to just be. If you need something large moved from here to there, a friend to listen and then give you the opposing view, or someone to cheer you on like it's inevitable that you'll succeed – ask the gentle giant. He also makes a mean kalimotxo and openly adores his wife, Kelli. He's the newest member writing in the Terranavis Universe and the author of The Adventures of Finnegan Dragonbender and The Lone Valkyrie (which is a continuation of Mila's story).

-Martha Carr

1. What turns you on?
Intelligence/ability to carry conversation (because I'm more likely to carry the plague than a conversation.)

2. What turns you off?

An inability to see fault in oneself. We all have short-comings, but if you can't admit that, then I don't want to be your friend.

3. Who do you most admire? Why?

This is a hard question... I admire a lot of people, but who do I admire most? Probably either my wife, or Martha.

4. What profession other than your own would you like to attempt?

Mechanical Engineering. I have most of a degree in it, but writing became a thing before I could actually finish. I love the idea of figuring out how things work and making them better.

5. What profession would you not like to do?

Anything that puts me in a cubicle for eight hours a day. I can't take cubicles; too much like a coffin.

6. If heaven exists, what would you like to hear God say when you arrive at the pearly gates?

God glances around to make sure no one can overhear, then leans in. "Look, I'm not really supposed to do this, but..." He cracks the gate open and pulls a pack of Marlboros from his robe. Tamping out a cigarette on the pack, he pops one between his lips, he gives me a wink before walking a few feet away and lighting up, turns his back to me and the open gate.

7. What is your favorite movie?

The Princess Bride. Greatest movie ever made. I'll fight you if you don't agree.

8. Who is your favorite character and from what book by which author?

Sazed from Mistborn Series by Brandon Sanderson.

9. What is something most people do not know about you?

I am VERY dyslexic. I also have a degree in Photography.

10. What do you look forward to most in the new year?

Getting my new book series out, along with a few audio books.

11. What's your favorite non-LMBPN series you've done? What's your favorite series inside LMBPN?

War Mage Chronicles and Adventures of Finnegan Dragonbender.

CONNECT WITH THE AUTHORS

TR Cameron Social

Website: www.trcameron.com

Facebook: https://www. facebook.com/AuthorTRCameron

Martha Carr Social

Website: http://www.marthacarr.com

Facebook: https://www.facebook.com/ groups/MarthaCarrFans/

Michael Anderle Social

Michael Anderle Social
Website:
http://www.lmbpn.com

Email List:
http://lmbpn.com/email/

Facebook Here: https://www.
facebook.com/TheKurtherianGambitBooks/